The Actor

by

Savannah Addison

The Actor

Cover Art by *Angela Anderson*

The Wild Rose Press, Inc.
PO Box 708
Adams Basin, NY 14410-0708
Visit us at www.thewildrosepress.com

Publishing History
First Yellow Rose Edition, 2017
Print ISBN 978-1-5092-1407-5
Digital ISBN 978-1-5092-1408-2

Published in the United States of America

Looking back at her,

seeing her lost in her thoughts, he had the sudden urge to do anything to make her happy, which was why he agreed to the worst idea she had proposed since he had arrived at her place weeks ago.

"Okay," he called back.

"Okay what?" she asked, forgetting what she'd suggested.

"Okay. We can jump our horses."

She smiled.

"Just let me say a few prayers first. Then dismount. Get a running start. After that, I will jump whatever horse you ask me to."

"Always the comedian," she said.

"My critics would disagree with you," he called back, thrilled that he had been able to amuse her. Just this once.

Dedication

To all the romantics,
those who proudly proclaim their love
for the saccharine to all who will listen
and those who read their favorite books
in a closet with a flashlight,
this is for you.

Chapter One

Colton Grey eyed his publicist, Moira Easton, one of the best in the business, as she gripped the steering wheel of the seafoam-green truck she was using to transport him to her cousin's farm. Her knuckles were white, her lips pursed, her brow knitted. An array of facial expressions flitted across her features, her mouth moving steadily, but silently.

Colton could recognize the signs. Moira was weighing the pleasure she often derived from lecturing him about his unwise decisions and related bad behavior against the obvious lack of benefit—he had yet to change in response to even a single one of her tirades.

Still, she must have needed some form of release because giving the lecture won out.

"So, let's review what we've learned, shall we?" she asked.

It was clear her statement was rhetorical. Everything about her body language said they would be reviewing whatever she wished. Her use of the royal *we* punctuated that fact.

Colton fought against his hangover, hoping he could perform as he was supposed to. He didn't want to induce a round of shrieking in Moira. She hadn't shrieked before, not that he could remember. But sometimes, when her face went really red, he thought she might lose it and devolve into a blob with spinning head, bulging eyes, and all manner of theatrical accompaniments to boot.

"So, what are you going to do?" she asked.

"Stay sober," Colton answered.

"And what are you not going to do?"

"Try to seduce your cousin."

"And if you break said rules?"

"You will castrate me and feed me to the lions in the San Diego Zoo."

"Excellent. We are on the same page."

The beat-up truck that Moira had secured to drive them from Los Angeles to her cousin's farm in an unknown town in barely known Idaho puttered along as Colton stared out the window.

He couldn't pinpoint when one drink had become one drink too many or when he transitioned from alcohol to substances far worse for him. But against his better judgment, he had.

Now, thanks to an array of recent transgressions in public and in private, Colton's involvement in a major movie franchise had been put on hold. He had three months to sober up and demonstrate that he could stay on the straight and narrow. Three months. Approximately ninety days.

Colton had already tried the traditional route. But his recent stay in a rehab facility was ineffectual for several reasons. For one, he'd traded his addiction to alcohol and drugs for an addiction to women. This had not gone over well, especially since his most notable seduction had included the activities director at the rehab center, an activities director who was currently on a leave of absence for conduct unbecoming a psychology professional. If she had been licensed, Colton's behavior probably would have damaged her life even further—she would have been disbarred or delicensed or whatever happens to higher-ups in the field of psychology when they fail to uphold the ethical guidelines of their profession.

Second, after his attempt to kiss and fondle his way out of any potential withdrawal pains, he had started an alcohol- and drug-procuring service. Namely, he had called a buddy, snuck out of the facility whose security was a joke because no one wanted to tick off the rich, famous, and well-connected clientele housed within, and had returned with cartons of cigarettes, liters of alcohol, and an array of pills and powders, only some of which he could name. He had been thrown out for that. Unceremoniously.

Third, news of his indiscretions had circulated far and wide. By way of general gossip, breaking news, print headlines, and tabloid speculation, treatment facilities across the country, even the world, had been well informed of the cons that accompanied his pros.

"He is a danger to the progress of our other clients," one rehab facility had said.

"He is a threat to our staff," another had echoed.

"We don't care how much potential he has," a third had argued. "His actions show that he is not ready to get better."

After all of the most reputable treatment centers had said no, Colton had watched as Moira had moved on to other options. Her success in the business had proven she wasn't used to being denied. She was known far and wide for her ability to bring famous producers to tears during negotiations.

Still, even Colton had been surprised when she had turned her laser focus on getting him better and back at the head of his acting class. He'd never seen her get so creative; her opponent, his ever-tricky, ever-shifting, ever-slippery addiction, was to thank for that.

And it was Moira's creativity that Colton had to thank for the month or more he had to spend drying out on his publicist's cousin's farm. His location for the remainder of the two months he had to remain sober had yet to be determined. Moira had said it all depended on his behavior.

Colton knew he could deal with the hayfields that would be present on the farm. Acres and acres of hayfields. Those were standard. Or so it seemed, based on the few movies that he had watched about life on a farm.

But he couldn't tolerate cows. Not their mooing nor their grazing nor their refuse.

And he, especially, could not tolerate chickens.

God, please don't let there be any chickens, he thought.

Ever since starring in a film where the surprise killer was a psychotic, larger-than-life chicken, he'd had trouble even looking at one of the birds.

There are only so many times you can have your heart mechanically pecked out by an animatronic version of the gallus gallus domesticus *before you no longer want to see the culprit that did it.*

Colton laughed to himself at the thought.

"What? What are you laughing at?" Moira asked. Her tone revealed that she was at the end of her rope. It was clear to him that she, like everyone else, had had it with a certain Mr. Colton Grey. In fact, he was sure, if he weren't her most successful client, she would have dumped him on the side of the road by now.

"Nothing," he said. "I was thinking about how much I hate chickens."

"Right. Well, you're going to have to deal. Haven's place has chickens."

"What?" He turned in his seat to eye her accusingly. "You promised there wouldn't be chickens."

"I lied. Big deal," she answered. "You should be used to it by now."

This was true. She had lied and told him rehab would be fun. She had lied and said she could find him a new facility to stay at, one with an ocean view perhaps. He should have predicted she would lie about the accommodations down on the family farm.

When will the lies stop, he wondered, knowing, of everybody in his life, he had told the biggest lies of all.

"You mind if I turn on the radio?"

"Be my guest," Moira answered.

Colton hadn't listened to music in months, unless forced to. Ever since his break-up with a very public pop star, he hadn't had a taste for the stuff. The rumor was he drank because she had cheated and left. The truth of the matter was she left because he drank.

Neither had cheated though. Cheating wasn't something he could do. He was committed to all things in his life, good and bad, once he was in. The problem was he'd gone in on some pretty bad stuff. And stepped out of the good arena far too long ago.

Movies had looked less appealing as liquid hope and powdered confidence had called to him more and more.

Having your best friend date your ex-girlfriend could do that to a guy.

Now, he felt hopeless. His private struggles were public. And his demons were the size of the billboards on Hollywood Boulevard.

"How long 'til we're there?"

"A few more hundred miles."

"Tell me again why we didn't take a plane?"

"Because you would be recognized on a plane. And because they serve tiny glass bottles in first class."

"Right."

"Where did you get the booze last night?"

"A flask in my suitcase."

"I thought I emptied it."

"You did. I refilled it."

Colton enjoyed what was sure to be only a silent minute or two before Moira chastised him again.

"You do realize the future of your career is on the line?"

"Yes," he muttered.

"You were a child star. One of the best." She dug her thumb into the steering wheel. "Now, you are transitioning. This is a key time."

"Save it, Moira. I've heard the lectures before."

From family. From friends. Everybody, it seemed, was concerned with his bottom line. Everybody except the one person who truly mattered.

Never mind, a girl is a girl is a girl, he told himself. *They all have the same parts.*

They should have been interchangeable.

Except they weren't. Which was the problem.

Colton couldn't get Anna Robbie out of his head. She was the first girl he'd loved. She was the one who'd introduced him to the nightlife. Then, she'd left him because of it.

Ironic, he thought. Once upon a time, he was too straitlaced for her. She'd had to loosen him up. Encourage him to live it up.

Now, it seemed, she was too straitlaced for him. Kind of a joke really, since pop stars and rendezvous with nasty little habits in dark rooms were practically synonymous.

As Colton turned his attention back to the landscape speeding by, his ex's most recent number one hit wafted through the dilapidated speakers in the beat-up ol' truck.

Instead of screaming or changing the channel, he did something new.

He gave life to the question that had been swirling around his head since the world's most recently crowned princess of pop had ended things with him.

He wondered to himself, *Anna. Why did you let me go?*

Chapter Two

Colton's head pounded as Moira cheerfully announced that they'd arrived.

"And you thought we would never get here," she added.

Colton harrumphed as he rolled out of the truck, landing directly in a pile of horse manure.

"Nice," Moira said as she came to his side of the vehicle, setting his luggage, a collection of expensive canvas duffel bags, on the ground.

"Just add expert comedic timing to my list of ever-growing talents," he said, as he scraped his shoe off on a nearby pile of chopped logs.

Colton Grey had been sober for less than twenty-four hours, which was twenty-four hours too many.

If there weren't a ten-million-dollar payday slated for the first of three films in a series anticipated to gross billions on the line, he'd be out of here. But he hadn't been born with a silver spoon in his mouth. Not like Anna. He'd had to work for everything he'd gotten.

"You okay?" Moira studied his face closely.

His dark thoughts must have been apparent on his face, rolling across his features like storm clouds across a gloomy sky.

"Sure. Fine. I'm fine," he said.

Sobriety, so far, is not a pretty color on me.

But he'd learn to wear it more demurely. He had

to. Moira Easton of the take-no-prisoners Eastons had ordered it.

"Okay, then. Let's go find my cousin."

"What's her name again?"

"Haven," Moira's cousin answered, coming around a corner. "Haven Morrow."

There was a reason Moira had warned him off of her cousin. She was gorgeous. Not in the starlet, I-primp-because-I-can kind of way either. She was naturally pretty. Stunning without a lick of makeup on.

And with what he hoped was a mud smear on her jeans, not more horse refuse.

"Colton. Colton Grey," he offered, mimicking her James Bond way of introducing herself. "Nice to meet you."

Haven briefly accepted his extended hand, shook it softly, then dropped it so she could give her cousin a hug.

"Moira! It's so good to see you."

"Same to you," his publicist said. "How's your—"

But Haven cut her off. "What have you been up to in good ol' Los Angeles?"

There was a story behind whatever Moira was going to inquire about. A good one, Colton thought.

"You know, keeping the riffraff in line." She gestured to Colton.

For his part, he looked every bit as unashamed as he wanted others to think he felt. It wasn't like he had been the first Hollywood actor to slide down the slippery slope of alcohol and substance abuse.

"What's there to do around here?" Colton asked, interrupting their conversation.

"A whole lot of nothing," Haven replied.

"That's why you're here," Moira added.

"Where's the nearest town?"

"About a hundred miles either way," his publicist's cousin answered. "The ones with anything fun to do anyway."

A hundred miles? What kind of hellhole has Moira dragged me to?

As Colton searched for the words that would get him back into the truck and away from the deserted corner of Earth on which he stood, Moira handed over an envelope full of money to Haven and gave her the number for the burner cell phone that she had purchased, so she could be regularly updated regarding Colton. She explained to Haven that they would all be using untraceable cell phones, so that the paparazzi couldn't pay anybody off to find Colton's whereabouts.

"Better to be safe than sorry," Moira said. "Be good," she added as she shot back to the truck. "I apologize for having to run, but I'll see you both soon. In three months."

So much for discussing where I will be spending the second and third month of my forced sobriety, Colton thought.

He watched as Moira drove down the long, windy lane that had brought him to the farmhouse where he'd just been introduced to her cousin, his new keeper.

"So…?" Haven asked.

Colton could feel her eyes taking him in, assessing his mood.

"So," he said, mimicking her.

"Would you like a grand tour?"

"More than one that isn't grand," he answered, knowing his joke was lame. But he was running on fumes here, the synthetic energy he'd been using for the last several months having recently been taken from him.

"Okay. Let's get started. The farm is big. We'll start with the buildings and fields near the house. Tomorrow, we can drive you around to see the rest if you like."

"Sure. Fine. Sounds good," he said, reminding himself that only one answer had been necessary. Not three.

Haven led him toward the house, carrying one of his bags. He tried to grab it from her, but she refused to relinquish it.

"We call it hospitality out here in the sticks," she said, as she walked up the front steps of a modestly sized residence. She led him around the porch to the back, then back down another set of stairs.

Guess I'm not staying in the big house then, he thought.

"We have a guesthouse," she answered.

Maybe he'd said that out loud. "Did I...?" he asked, believing himself to be off to a particularly bad start, stepping in *it* figuratively and literally.

"No," she answered. "You just look confused."

"Oh. Okay. Good."

"Your fits of cursing and surly remarks have been for your ears only, so far."

He smiled at that. She knew exactly how happy he was to be here, which, of course, was not happy at all. "So, do you like movies?" he asked, sounding as stereotypical as possible.

"No," she answered, no shame in her voice.

"Like not at all?"

"Like not at all."

"Is this an Idaho thing?"

"Nope. It's a me thing. And here we are," she announced, a little too brightly.

So far, what he knew about the girl was that she was good at avoiding questions. Not subtle, but effectual.

This trip might be interesting after all. Moira might have sworn him off seducing her cousin. But that didn't mean he couldn't figure her out. After all, he had nothing else better to do.

Chapter Three

After a quick tour of his bunk, which was quite literally one of a set of stackable bunks, Haven directed him outside into the yard. According to her, the farmhouse was positioned at the center of the property, which meant that he was surrounded by a perimeter of plants, animals, or both.

"How many acres do you have?" Colton asked.

"Thousands," she answered.

"Your family must be wealthy then."

"We are land rich and cash poor," she said, leading him down to what appeared to be a barn.

"Do you ride?" she asked as her pace quickened, excitement pouring out of her.

Girls and their horses. He shook his head. "I have ridden, yes. I had to. For a movie. You know, that type of entertainment you don't like."

She ignored his jab. "Great. Then you can help me ride the fences in a couple of weeks."

"Ride the fences?"

"Look for any repairs that need to be made. Make sure the cows are okay. It's an old cowpoke term for anything that needs to be checked on out in the pastures."

"Oh. Right. Well, I never learned to herd cattle."

"It's not hard. It's routine for them now. They mostly herd themselves. Except for the stubborn ones."

Suddenly, the family resemblance was clear. Like Moira, Haven was not accustomed to taking no for an answer.

"Are there other chores I will be doing?" he asked, becoming aware that his stay was going to be less like the vacation he had imagined and more like the punishment that most everyone in his life thought he deserved.

"Moira told me to keep you busy, and a farm can always use an extra set of hands." She said the last part in what sounded like an apologetic tone.

Interesting.

Colton kept the conversation going because there were some things that Haven, his newest taskmaster, needed to know. "I think this would be a good time to mention that I have never, not once, helped any livestock give birth."

She nodded her head, taking in what he'd said.

"Also, I don't like chickens," he added quickly.

He'd found it was best to be short and to the point with any less-than-typical aversions. At least, that's what people did where he came from. *My name is Jym. That's J-Y-M. I am a peach-loving fruitarian, and I refuse to be exposed to the number seven.*

"Chickens?" Haven asked incredulously, snapping Colton back to the present.

The pair stood in the middle of the barn now with a couple of hay bales piled high at either end. Horses of all shapes and sizes occupied the available stalls.

Land and animal rich, he thought. *My dream come true.*

Haven looked at him, waiting for an answer.

"I starred in a movie once that had a psychotic,

murdering chicken in it. It was huge. Killed everyone in town. It ate my heart out actually."

"That's…gross," she responded.

No artifice to her reply at all.

He couldn't help but laugh. "Yeah. It kind of was. But I was new to the industry then. You either start in horror, or you play the sweet, innocent child that complicated parents or difficult circumstances screw up."

"I would have gone for the complicated parents, I think. Or the difficult circumstances."

"I didn't look innocent enough," he replied. "Not even then."

The corners of Haven's mouth turned up at the end. But when he flashed her his mega-watt smile, she immediately shut down.

"So, here are all of our horses," she said, gesturing. "You are free to ride anyone except the stallion, the pregnant mare, and Cicero. The stallion because no one can stay on him for longer than a few minutes. The pregnant mare because, as you can see, she's pregnant. And Cicero because he is mine.

"Mine and mine alone," Haven crooned to the palomino gelding as she scratched him behind the ears. The golden animal leaned into her touch before reaching past her caress toward her back pocket.

"All right," she said. "One sugar cube."

Within a second, she produced a small, white crystalline square. Once it was officially offered to him, the horse lipped it up eagerly.

Suddenly, Colton was uncomfortable. Like really uncomfortable. He was not used to wanting to be a horse. But the draw of the sugar cube, that was familiar.

Only, in his mind, it was something far more potent.

Palms sweaty and heart racing, he broke the silence. "I am happy to avoid riding unless forced," he said, because he needed to derail his own unhealthy thoughts. And because he had no idea how to bear witness to such a sweet, simple moment as the one before him: horse and rider exchanging mutual affection.

"No problem," Haven answered. "I'll just have to force you."

With anybody else, that statement would have been a form of flirting. But with Haven, it was different.

She didn't gauge his every reaction like Anna once did.

She didn't try to secure his attention like the groupies who used to stand outside his hotel room, screaming his name for days.

She didn't seem to be after anything. Not like the few special fans who were invited to get to know him more intimately. One of the many nails in his figurative coffin.

Soon, he and the girl with an unpolished air were walking again. Colton was trying to focus on what she was saying, but her behavior had him flummoxed. He wasn't used to being…normal. Not anymore.

"I won't introduce you to the chickens," she said as they continued their tour. "But I will show you where they are so you can give them a wide berth."

He chuckled. She was teasing him. It had been years since he'd been teased so innocently.

He could picture the list of facts she was assembling about him.

Colton does not like chickens. Check. Colton will

be giving them a wide berth. Check. Colton is an idiot. Double check.

So that she didn't add lazy ignoramus to the list, he ran to catch up with her. The girl may be short, but she sure could move when she walked.

"Do you mind if I ask how old you are?" he questioned.

"Seventeen. Almost eighteen. My birthday is in a few weeks."

"And you run a farm?"

"Sure. Someone has to."

"What about school? Did you graduate early?"

"I am being home-schooled."

Like me, he thought, though he'd graduated early at sixteen.

"Isn't this a little much for a seventeen-year-old?" he asked, gesturing to the expanse around him.

"My dad is dead. My mom is…busy," she answered, her voice strained. "And my brother isn't here."

"You have a brother?"

"See that shed over there?" she asked, gesturing to an enormous building.

"Yes," he responded, though there seemed to be several identical buildings bunched together.

"That is where the chickens reside."

He could feel the familiar tingle on the underside of his hands, sense the excited numbness running itself up his arms in short spurts.

"How many chickens do you have exactly?" he asked, his voice giving way, revealing a slight stutter.

"I've lost count," she answered, probably more for effect than anything else.

It appeared she was making fun of his fear, aware that if she implied that she didn't know the exact number, there would be no way she could make sure that a few hadn't escaped.

He vowed to get her back when the time was right.

"The cows are all in their pastures," she continued. "They're only brought up here for shots, for birthing if we think there is going to be an issue, and for sale."

"You sell your cows?"

"This is a working farm, Mr. Grey. Of course, we sell them."

He nodded his head, amused that she had referred to him by his last name.

Anna would have been outraged at his proximity to "animal cruelty." Her hot, vegan, pleather-wearing self would have started a march right here and now. She'd have spray painted Haven's boots and thrown glitter or fake blood or whatever else PETA protesters threw on their targets.

Colton, for his part, was kind of impressed with Haven. He had his own checklist about her going on in his head.

Gumption. Check. Runs a farm by herself. Check. Remains unimpressed by me. Double check.

Colton thought he might find he liked this Haven character after all.

Chapter Four

"Time to wake up," Haven called through the screen of the bunkhouse in which Colton was staying.

He rubbed sleep from his eyes, thought about getting up for a second, then rolled over and went back to bed.

"Colton. You have to get up," Haven repeated.

"It's..."

"Six-thirty. I know. I let you sleep in."

Sleep in, he thought, incredulous. *What kind of hours do farmers keep?*

Early morning was usually when he was settling into sleep, not awakening from it. Of course, that seemed to be a thing of the past now, a relic of a time when he had been allowed to have a say in his own life.

"I just need a minute."

"Grab a quick shower, then meet me on the porch. I have some breakfast for you. After you finish that, we are going to work in the barn."

This girl had a serious working problem. Like she did too much of it.

Colton was used to getting up early for the occasional photo shoot at dawn or for early morning roll calls for a film. But no barns had ever been involved. And with the exception of that chicken horror movie and the flick in which he had had to ride a horse, livestock and anything that resembled it had been kept

19

far, far away from his sleep-derived eyes.

Consequently, he couldn't imagine he was going to be of much use to anybody for at least a few more hours. Not without a hit of something uplifting.

Still, he didn't want Moira flying in to chew him out within a day of his arrival. She would have made him pay for that. In more ways than one.

So, Colton got out of bed. After stumbling around for a minute, trying to get his bearings, he grabbed his towel, exited the bunkhouse, and walked along the porch to the back of the building where the showers and restrooms were. He supposed it made sense for the restrooms to be easily accessible from the outside since most farm people were not in a building most of the day. But it felt a bit like a campground.

A campground without readily accessible marshmallows, he thought. *Or hot cocoa. The worst kind.*

After a quick, cold shower and a speedy shave that left his face looking like it had recently collided with the pavement and gone for a skid, Colton emerged from his lodgings. He jogged over to where Haven was standing, a napkin-wrapped sandwich in her hand.

"Here you go. Chicken biscuit."

This permutation of a chicken, he liked. He had no problem with the feathery creature in its proper form—as a meal.

"Thanks," he mumbled after a rather large bite.

She handed him a cup of orange juice and signaled that there was a coffee that awaited him once he was done with that.

"It's black. If you want cream and sugar, I can go add some."

"No. Black is fine," he answered.

He wanted to ask her if she had made the food. He had this image of her harvesting all of the ingredients by hand, rolling out the biscuits, squeezing the orange juice. He hadn't seen any coffee trees yet, but one never knew. There were thousands of acres after all.

As quickly as he could, Colton finished his sandwich. He downed the rest of his orange juice and then grabbed his coffee.

"So, what are we up to?" he asked.

"The stalls need to be completely mucked out, then filled back in with sawdust."

That's not too bad, he thought. He'd had to muck a stall before. With a crew watching and he'd had the day to do it. But still, it was something he was familiar with.

"Then, we need to go through the hay. Get rid of whatever is moldy. We had a leak in the roof recently."

He nodded his head. Still doable.

Then, she rattled off another four or five chores before saying, "After that, we'll grab lunch before starting on the afternoon chores."

Say what? he thought to himself. *She expects that we will get all of this done before noon?*

Instead of complaining, he focused on keeping up with her. He didn't want to appear incapable. He may have been a slightly pampered city boy, but that didn't make him useless.

Once in the barn, Haven handed him a pitchfork and secured him a wheelbarrow.

"Take it all out. When the wheelbarrow gets full, you can dump it over there," she instructed, pointing at a very large brownish heap a good distance away from the barn.

"Then sprinkle the floor with this white powder. It's lye. It will remove the smell of urine."

He nodded his head.

"Don't get it on you. It burns."

Another nod.

"We'll fill the stalls back in later. I want them to air out for a bit first."

Colton stared down the rows of stalls. All of the horses had been put somewhere, a pasture no doubt.

"You think you can handle that?"

The way she said it made him sound less intelligent than the pitchfork against which he leaned. She must have registered his surprise because she immediately tempered her tone. "What I mean is, do you feel comfortable with me leaving you here to work on this?"

"Yes," he responded, smiling.

"Great," she said and trotted out of the barn and into the ever-brightening day.

"One," Colton counted to himself as he threw a huge heap of sawdust mixed with animal refuse into the wheelbarrow.

"Two," he said as he tossed another shovelful in, determined to figure out how much muck he was getting rid of.

After the third wheelbarrowful, he settled for a lot. Each stall had a lot. And each load was heavy.

His hands were starting to blister. He should have asked Haven if she had any more gloves like the ones he had seen tucked into her back pocket. That would have been smart, helpful.

Sweat dripping, Colton wiped his forehead and shoveled some more.

An hour and a half later, Haven dropped off some

ice water for him along with a pair of gloves. "I forgot these," she said. "Sorry."

He gratefully slipped them on, trying to obscure the angry red and white bubbles forming on his hands.

"It gets better," she said. "Once you are used to it."

He nodded his head and got back to work. He had no desire to have a conversation with a girl, especially one like Haven, about exactly how untough he was.

He'd made a career out of being the cinematic badass after all. The fact that he couldn't leap tall buildings in a single bound was not something he wanted getting out to his fan base.

After a few more minutes, his cell phone rang.

"Hello," he answered, knowing exactly who it was.

"Colton. Hi. How's it going?" Moira asked.

"Good," he answered, making her work for the information she was calling to procure.

"So, still…"

"Sober? Yes. We are approaching two days now." He threw his fist in the air in mock triumph. "Woo hoo!"

Moira appeared to see straight through him. "Baby steps, Colton. Remember what your providers at the treatment facility said."

"About that?" he asked. "How exactly am I supposed to attend an AA meeting? I don't think any of the horses here have a drinking problem, despite what the contents of their stalls might suggest."

"We are using a slightly different model," Moira answered hesitantly.

"Yes. The isolate-and-interrogate version of getting sober. You should write a book about it."

"Already secured a contract," she said, clearly

recognizing where this conversation was headed and not wanting to give in to his woe-is-me banter.

After an uncomfortable silence, he said what he should have said a while ago. "Seriously. Thanks for caring, Moira. I know I've been…"

"No problem, Colton. Gotta go. That's the director calling to see how you're doing. Don't want him to worry." With a click, she was off the phone.

Colton returned his mind to the task at hand.

Two stalls later, he realized what he was doing now and what Moira did for a living were surprisingly pretty similar.

Chapter Five

"You did great today," Haven told Colton as they walked toward the farmhouse from the barn.

"Thanks," he responded, bone-tired.

"Dinner will be ready in an hour."

Colton nodded his head. He had no intention of staying up long enough to eat a meal. He wanted to shower and hit the hay. Not the kind he was sorting through and arranging all day either. He wanted to be reacquainted with the figurative variety.

"Come up when you're ready," she added as she headed toward her home.

Colton walked into the bunkhouse. He stripped off his shirt and threw it onto the pile he had created in the corner. Then he stripped off his jeans, grabbed a towel, and headed back outside toward the showers.

During the main harvest, the bunkhouse was reportedly full. But he had it all to himself right now, which was a good thing. He couldn't imagine being surrounded by rough-and-tumble strangers at this particular juncture in his life.

Certainly not salt-of-the-earth types. They wouldn't understand the urge to use that was tugging at Colton's veins.

It's been a long day, the voice said.

You've earned it, another whisper urged.

Craving had become a part of him. With many

voices and their equally plentiful reasons to procure just one more taste of the good stuff talking over each other in his head all day, every day.

Before, he'd dabbled. Now, all of the dabbling he did was in sobriety. A day here, a day there was all he could tolerate of the uninebriated world.

A shower, he thought to himself. *I'll feel better after a shower.*

He was at the moment-to-moment stage of getting well. He couldn't tolerate a full twenty-four-hour commitment to the right path.

Colton stepped into the shower, which was essentially a closet with a drain. Once the door was closed behind him, he removed his boxers and tossed them onto a small wooden bench too covered in soap scum to sit on. Then he turned his face up to the water. It was warm, unlike before. Haven must have fixed the pipe or turned on the water heater or something.

The girl was handy. He would give her that.

Colton knew he should hurry, get ready, offer to help make dinner, and sit down to eat with Haven. Return the hospitality she had shown him somehow. But he could barely move. His muscles were sore. His blistered hands stung. His shoulders were drawn up around his neck, the muscles there as knotted as they had ever been.

The longer he stood in the stream of water, the better he started to feel. It wasn't long before ten minutes gave way to thirty, then to an hour.

Eventually, he forced himself out. A quick turn of the handle and he was greeted by less than steamy air, his hot water having run out a bit ago, no lingering warmth to heat him.

Colton reached for a pair of clean boxers to slide on before realizing he had never grabbed a pair.

Crap.

Wrapping the towel around his middle, he stepped out onto the bunkhouse's porch and ran straight into Haven.

"What the…?" he asked, scrambling for the towel that had loosened itself from his grip.

She didn't so much as flinch.

"Um, Haven? I need to get by."

"Right," she answered, looking closely at his face.

"Can I…?"

"Sure," she said, stepping out of the way, never once taking her eyes off him.

He could hear her muttering to herself as he hotfooted it toward the bunk. He yanked open the door, then closed it quickly, putting something between her and his unclad form. He was usually comfortable with nudity, semi or full. But not right now. Not with the way she was looking at him, as if she could see further into him than he had ever seen into himself.

She'd seemed so displeased.

Before she had the time to reappear out of nowhere, he grabbed a pair of clean boxers and tugged them on in the darkest corner of the room.

Then he stepped over to his suitcase to pick out something to wear to the dinner he had planned on ditching. Only, his clothes weren't arranged the way he'd had them prior. Someone had been looking through his things.

Is she spying on me?

Colton threw on a T-shirt and cotton pants, then headed back outside.

Haven remained on the porch, as close to the door to the sleeping area as possible.

"Did you go through my stuff?" he asked, anger rising in his voice.

She looked him dead in the eye and nodded her head.

"What gives you the right—?"

She held up his flask.

"Moira emptied that already. There was nothing in it."

She pulled another flask from behind her back. And with it a plastic baggie full of pills. He had stashed them both in the underlining of his suitcase.

"You can't just go through someone's stuff like that," he barked, reaching for his loot.

It wasn't so much that he wanted it back. He just didn't want her to be holding it up at him as though she was a cop and he was the suspect. He was embarrassed like he had never been before.

"You're supposed to be getting clean," she responded, ice in her voice.

"I haven't used since I got here," he countered.

"So, these were for in case?"

He looked to the side. He couldn't make eye contact. He wished she could understand. He'd practically forgotten he had the stuff.

Until right before my shower, he reminded himself. *I had been jonesing then.*

"Tell me. Truthfully," she continued. "How many have you taken?"

Colton's back was up now. He wasn't used to answering to anybody. He'd been on his own for a while.

He stared her down, willing her to back off, to learn the place she had in his life, which was nowhere. She stared him down right back.

After a bit, he finally answered. "None, okay? I haven't used any. I was planning to…but then I got here…and I just didn't, all right? I haven't used in a couple of days."

"A couple? Addicts know the exact time they last used."

"Two. Two days. I haven't used since I got drunk with the liquor in that flask. Before Moira dropped me off. The day before she dropped me off. I was hungover most of the way here."

The specificity did little to soothe her, even if the doubt in her eyes had receded.

Haven took one step closer. She was now inches from his face. She looked up into his eyes and said, "If you lie to me, you are out of here. I won't go through this. Not again."

At her admission, her eyelids fluttered. She hadn't meant to reveal anything about herself.

Colton was eager to know more. She'd gone through this before. With someone she cared about, not a stranger. "Who?" he asked.

She ignored his question. "You swear this is the last of it?"

He could have lied. She probably would have never found it. But the look on her face plus her earnestness convinced him differently. He didn't ever want to be the reason for the pain he saw in her eyes right then.

So, he walked back into the bunk, grabbed his shiny black oxfords, twisted the heel on the left shoe, and caught the sachet of the best cannabis he'd ever smoked as it fell out of its secret compartment. Then he twisted the heel of the right one, grabbed its contraband contents, and headed back out to the porch.

Once he was standing next to Haven again, he handed her two baggies—one full of dried brown leaves, the other full of small, white, perfectly oval pills. His favorite downer.

"That's the last of it," he answered.

And it was.

They both retreated to their separate corners, settling into a temporary truce.

Chapter Six

Colton lay in bed, but he couldn't sleep. He was furious. At himself.

A girl who didn't know him from Adam prior to his arrival had opened her home to him and how had he repaid her? By bringing up painful memories of her past?

He couldn't have known, of course. It wasn't like Moira had given him a travel guide and pointed out the dos and don'ts of interacting with the wildlife on this farm, of which Haven was the main attraction.

No. Moira had told him to behave. And he hadn't managed to do even that. He should have dumped out the drugs the first chance he'd gotten. Instead, he'd held on to them.

What was the saying? Addicts want more, now, and again.

And that's what he was. No matter what he told others. He was an addict.

He may not have ever experienced delirium tremens or soiled his own pants during an episode of withdrawal, but his mind wanted—no, craved—drugs as a crutch.

At the thought, Colton rolled over and screamed into his pillow. The lumpy form atop his bed did what it was supposed to do. It muffled the sound.

I've made a mess of my life, he admitted, if only to

himself.

In interview after bloody interview, he'd sworn he would never travel the road of many a child star before him. No drugs, he'd promised. No alcohol in excess. No partying beyond harmless, industry get-togethers and the occasional, tame after-party.

And now, here he was on a farm in the middle of nowhere because he couldn't be trusted in rehab. Rehab was a place that welcomed the lost and the hopeless. But even those accustomed to the lies and the broken promises that come with getting sober recognized that Colton Grey wasn't a good bet.

They saw him as standing at the apex of his spiral. They knew he had many more rock-bottoms ahead of him if he applied himself, or failed to apply himself, as the case may be.

Colton used to argue that he couldn't be addicted because he didn't use every day. But his binges were regular enough to be part of a pattern and, most importantly, to do harm.

He'd done so many people so much harm. As they had him.

Anna?

He missed the girlfriend who had treated him like dirt once he found himself knee-deep in his current difficulties. Normal people didn't miss the fair-weather type. He knew he should move on. Yet whenever he started traipsing down memory lane, hers was the face that rose to the top, floating above all others.

Tap, tap, tap.

Colton looked up at the sound. Through the screen door, he could see Haven. She had a steaming mug in her hand.

"Can I come in?" she asked.

He wondered what she'd witnessed. His screams? His wallowing? The self-pity that wafted off of his frame, rising from his skin in swirls?

He sat up, laid his arms over his bent knees, and nodded yes, his voice a nonentity at the moment.

She brought the mug over to him. "It's herbal tea."

He took the warm beverage, but didn't say thank you.

"I want to apologize," she began.

He looked at her now, noticing the tension that pulled at one side of her mouth.

"I know it must feel weird to know that I went through your stuff," she continued.

"It does."

"I just thought, when you didn't show up for dinner, that maybe…"

"I was using?"

"Yes."

"So you went through my stuff?"

"Yes."

"And now you are sorry that you did?"

"Not exactly," she said, revealing the complex nature of her apology. "I am only sorry that, by going through your stuff, I made you uncomfortable."

He didn't respond, took a sip of his tea instead.

She stood up then, crossed the floor, smoothed out a few invisible wrinkles in one of the gray blankets on a bed on the far side of the room.

"May I ask you a question?" he asked, wanting to know something about her since it seemed that she knew so much about him.

"Depends on the question, I guess," she answered,

appearing to anticipate the information he sought.

"You said you've been through this before."

She smiled a sad smile. "Yes."

"Was it a boyfriend?"

She shook her head.

"A relative?"

No response.

"A friend?

"Perhaps," she answered.

"To which one?"

"To both," she replied. "And that's all you'll get out of me, I am afraid."

Her vulnerability was apparent. Colton had the sudden urge to stand up, put down his tea, and take her into his arms, tell her it would all be okay. That was what he would do if he were in a movie right now. "But I'm not," he whispered to himself.

"You're not what?"

He chuckled. Even his lips were betraying him. "I didn't mean to say that out loud."

When he failed to offer an explanation, she accepted his answer as the only one he would be giving.

As she headed for the door, she called back over her shoulder, "I hope tomorrow can be a new day."

Noting the quiver in her voice, he turned his full attention toward her, taking in her strength and her vulnerability. They existed in perfect proportion to each other.

She didn't flinch under his gaze. But after a bit, she prompted, "I think we would both benefit from a clean slate."

She was seeking his assent. She saw him as a full participant in this process, not a subject.

Following a deep sigh, he agreed, "Yeah. Okay. Tomorrow is a new day."

He didn't believe in clean slates. A man's past defined his present. But for now, he would give the idea a try.

Colton wouldn't mind if he was proven wrong. Not this time.

Chapter Seven

Colton threw a fifty-pound bag of grain onto the stockpile a few feet away.

Man, do cows eat a lot. And horses, too.

"You're doing well," Haven offered as she walked in with a plastic jug of sweet tea and a couple of mismatched, equally synthetic glasses.

"Now, I thought all tea was served in a glass pitcher. On a veranda. By people paid to attend to your every wish and whim."

"In the land of dreams maybe."

"Touché," he offered, as he walked over and took a swig.

Within seconds, he was spitting out the beverage. "What is this? Liquid sugar?"

"It's called sweet tea."

"This isn't sweet. This is deadly."

"What are you saying? That I don't know how to make good tea?"

"I am saying you would be shot for serving this where I come from. A fructaphobe just got her wings in LA."

"You don't have to drink it. There's water over there in that hose."

Hmm. She's a little put out.

Their clean slate was getting tarnished once again. It had been five days since she had found his stash, which meant he'd been sober for a week.

He needed to work on his manners. Haven had weathered many a sarcastic dig and unfair attack over the course of his stay despite the fact that he had been using his "skills" to keep himself in line.

Skills, my rear, he thought. *I don't have any skills. Not past smiling at the camera and doing what I'm told to do, saying what I'm told to say, moving how I'm told to move.*

He was an infant in a twenty-two-year-old's body. Or a toddler. Maybe a toddler. He didn't require diapers at this point in his life.

"Haven, I'm—"

She nodded her head. She always stopped him before an apology. It was clear that she'd heard "I'm sorry" one too many times with little changing afterward.

Knowing a moment of lightness was needed, he walked over to the hose.

"Colton, you don't really have to…"

But he didn't drink from the hose. He sprayed her instead, his thumb registering when the sun-warmed water gave way to a cool, refreshing stream. He'd be lying if he said he didn't relish the idea of the cool water sending a chill up her spine. She'd sent enough up his the past few days.

As she threw up her hands to protect her face, he did his best to form a spout that sent water arcing over and around her so she couldn't escape. He made sure not to get anything wet that would mold. He didn't think she'd be at all amused by that. Not in the slightest.

At first, Haven looked annoyed. Then she smirked.

Finally, she laughed. A carefree laugh that a record producer would tape and lay down on a track meant to further the career of a young nubile girl pretending to be a worldly woman. If only he could get his hands on such a thing.

How quickly we grow up in LA, he thought. *The children in the City of Angels are anything but.*

Eventually, Haven braved the stream and grabbed the hose from him. Colton didn't move as she soaked him like he had just soaked her. He even opened his mouth and drank as she suggested. The water was so much purer than what was served in the restaurants that he was used to visiting a thousand miles southwest. Purer still than that found in the bars he once frequented.

Just as Haven was really getting into drenching him, Colton's phone rang. It was probably Moira calling to congratulate him on his one-week anniversary. He signaled Haven to stop in such a way that she listened.

"Hello," he answered, pulling out his phone and wiping it on a towel hanging in the supply room at the end of the barn.

"Colton. Hi," a strange voice offered.

"Who is this?" Whoever it was, it wasn't Moira.

"This is Sun Daily from *Celeb4U*. How are you doing today?"

He didn't play along with the falsely pleasant tone. "How did you get this number?" he asked instead.

"I have my sources," the woman answered, a purr in her voice.

"Who is that?" Haven asked.

"Don't call here again," Colton barked, knowing he

would have to get rid of the phone. Moira would have to send another three untraceable cells only to have the numbers discovered again. It's what always happened. At least in his life.

Colton threw the phone on the ground and ground it with his heel. He was done with being the world's most recent riches-to-rags story. Well, riches to designer rags. He still had ample savings and a chance to earn back what he'd spent if only he could stick with his plan.

A plan he'd been buying into fully. Until, like now, the urge to use reared its ugly head.

"Colton? Who was that?"

"Sun Daily."

"Sun who?"

"Sun Daily. She works for *Celeb4U*. She's a reporter."

"What did she say?"

"She asked how I was doing."

"That isn't so b—"

"She knows, Haven. The whole world knows about my...problem. She was calling to see how badly I've failed this time."

"But you haven't failed," Haven countered. "You're doing great."

"Really? You think? Then tell me why all I want is a drink right now. And a hit of something uplifting."

"That's normal," she stated. "Everyone in recovery craves."

"Where'd you read that? A pamphlet?"

She ignored his jab. "It's normal for someone with a history of addiction, Colton. You're not the only one who has gone through something like this."

"Great. I'm normal."

"You have to focus on the positive. You're not drinking. That's all that matters."

"Not to the papers," he complained, running his fingers through his hair.

Haven busied herself with wrapping the now lifeless hose around its holder.

After a few deep breaths, he said he was sorry, then confessed in a much calmer voice, "I just want it all to go away."

"I know," she said, walking over to put her hand on his arm.

"I'm not talking about just the drinking."

She waited for him to continue.

"I'm sick of being a spectacle." He sighed. "I never thought I'd hate the fame…"

"But you do," she finished.

He nodded. No matter how long you knew what was coming, sometimes, when it arrived, it was bigger and worse than you could ever have imagined.

"I couldn't do what you do," Haven stated plainly. It was her attempt to bolster his confidence.

"What? Pretend for a living? It's not as hard as what you do."

"Face the constant mirror," she corrected.

He tilted his head at her.

"The whole world reflects back to you who you are. Except it's all distorted. Like funhouse mirrors. They show you who they see, not who you are."

He smiled a sad smile.

"That's a lot of information to have presented to you. Especially when none of it is true," she added.

"I don't know what's true anymore," he conceded.

"I do," she answered in her certain way.

"You do?"

"Yes. You're a good guy, Colton. A good guy who made a series of bad decisions. And I believe in you."

He took a step closer to her. Looking down, he noticed how green her eyes were. A color not found anywhere in nature except right before him. Moved by his own observation, Colton leaned down a bit. Haven's lips were attractive, too. Soft, supple, a pale pink. He could have kissed her then. He could have kissed her and forgotten all about what troubled him.

With a sharp intake of breath, both Colton and Haven took a step back. An image of a lion devouring him in the San Diego Zoo invaded his mind. He wasn't sure what picture overtook hers.

"I, uh…" He apologized and excused.

"Yes. Right…there's much to do."

"See you later, then?" He could barely keep his feet from flying out the barn door ahead of him as he retreated, not waiting for an answer.

"See you then," Haven called over her shoulder, also immersed in the need to be far, far away.

Stupid, Colton thought to himself as he reached the outside world. *Stupid. Stupid. Stupid. What in the hell was I thinking?*

A typically submerged voice of reason answered him back emphatically: *As usual, you weren't.*

For the rest of the day, Colton "Self-Destructive" Grey did his best to avoid Haven. As well as the thought of what Moira would do to him once he found out about their almost kiss.

Chapter Eight

Until he couldn't any longer.

With the new phone Moira had overnighted having rung nonstop in his pocket since it arrived, Colton finally accepted that he had to answer at least one of her calls, eventually, and tell her something other than that he needed a new phone, a message he had sent via carrier pigeon yesterday.

Actually, a message Haven must have sent because he had not had a device with which to send it.

"So, you tried to kiss my cousin," Moira, his ever-informed, ever-vigilant publicist accused as soon as he answered her call.

Colton paced back and forth in the barn, taking a break from cleaning saddles and sorting out the good bridles from those that needed to be replaced or, at the very least, have fresh bits or other parts added.

"I wouldn't say *tried*," he began, trying to find a way to spin the loudest nonevent this side of the biggest river in Idaho.

The Snake River? Or is that just the longest river in Idaho? I can't remember what whatyaknow.com said when I looked it up.

"What would you say, then?" Moira asked, snapping him back to the present. "You somehow stumbled forward and almost bumped teeth with her?"

Colton suppressed the urge to smile. The facial

expression, though hidden from her view by the miles between him, would have undoubtedly shown itself in his voice somehow. And that would not have helped the situation. Not at all.

Moira could be a fearsome beast when at her most calm. He would have preferred not to see her annoyance accelerating to speeds past Mach 10.

"I would say," he countered slowly, "that I almost, accidentally, touched my lips to her lips, sort of."

"That sounds very mature. Like you are taking full responsibility."

"It was a mistake, Moira. A moment of weakness. It won't happen again."

"It better not. I am not joking around, Colton. Not when it comes to Haven. She is better than you could ever hope to deserve."

The rebuke stung a little. It was meant to, and it should have. Still, no matter how true what Moira was saying happened to be, it hurt to know that someone was completely out of your league.

"The lion's name is Jagter," Moira added. "It means 'hunter' in Afrikaans."

"What are you talking about?" he asked, confused for a second.

"The head lion at the San Diego Zoo. The one who is licking his lips at the thought of tasting human flesh."

"You have been heard loud and clear, Moira. I assure you."

"I have him on speed dial. Unlike you, he will take my call any time of day or night."

"I've gotta go, Moira. Nice hearing from you. As usual."

He heard, "I'll be calling you this evening..."

shouted through the phone as he hung up.

He doubted Jagter was the lion's real name. Hunter was too convenient a meaning for the moniker of Moira's famed threat to possess. Still, he pictured what being fed to the lion in question might look like.

So, my dear Panthera leo. *It's nice to meet you. What sharp canines you have. I am to be your lunch. Would you like to start by devouring my phallus or my scrotum first? I am attached to both. So there isn't a choice that I would prefer you to make.*

"What's going on?" Haven asked, sneaking up on Colton once again.

He ignored her question and responded with a statement of his own. "You should be a spy. You're too stealthy for your own good."

"I don't think it's me," she defended herself. "I think it's you. You're clueless."

"Your talent does not my ineptitude make."

"Seriously, Colton, what's going on?"

She had been slightly argumentative and frequently short with him since their almost kiss. Apparently, he had messed up. Like really messed up.

By wanting her? By not kissing her? By being attracted to her kindness? Who knew?

If he couldn't understand himself, he knew he had absolutely no chance of understanding women. Not even a little bit. Not even for like five seconds.

"Moira called for her daily check-in," he answered, wanting to be separated from the products of his own mind.

"What did you tell her?" Haven sounded nervous.

"*I* didn't tell her anything."

"What is that supposed to mean?" she questioned,

sounding a bit more irritated than she had been for the last several days.

"It means that someone in this room told her about our almost kiss. And I don't think it was Cicero."

The gelding whinnied at the mention of his name. Haven reached out absentmindedly and patted his neck.

"It wasn't me, Colton."

"Then how does she know? Despite the fact that this is a working farm, I hardly ever see anyone else here. Delivery guys come and go. I can spot a few men in the fields on occasion. But there is no one else here. Just you, me, a woman in your house who I assume is your mother because she is the only other person from your life that fits the description, and a bunch of smelly horses, cows, and chickens."

"Don't insult the animals just because you're mad."

"Why not? They can't understand me."

"No. But I can. In case you've forgotten, I've opened my house up to you. And I've been a pretty good friend in the process."

It was the word *friend* that stopped him. He hadn't thought of Haven as a friend before now. As a girl, yes. A beautiful girl at that. But not a friend. He wasn't used to having friends. Even Moira, as caring as she was, got something from her relationship with him. A paycheck and the chance to make more money by dropping his name.

And Anna was never a friend. She had been something more than that. And something less. Always more and certainly less.

"Look, Haven, I'm sorry." Colton was getting used to apologizing now. He did it almost every day. What step was making amends? Eight? Nine? He was making it a part of steps one through twelve, *Big Book* be damned. "I've been on edge since—well, you know since what..." He sighed. "I shouldn't have tried...It was wrong...You were there...and..."

Great. Now, not only did he look like an asshole and walk like an asshole, he talked like an asshole.

"Colton, I'm the one who should be sorry," Haven interrupted. Again with the unpredictable responses. "I was only trying to encourage you, and I blurred a line. It's my fault really. I know what you're dealing with."

"Haven, really, I am the one who stepped closer to you..."

"I said it's my fault. I should have watched my words."

Though he wanted to scream inside at the kid-glove handling, he didn't argue. He was tired of arguing. Tired of disagreements in general. And threats and cajoling and everything else that was a fixed part of an addict's life.

Instead, he remained silent. Not moody silent. Just silent. It was a new state for him, his mind blank rather than on go.

Haven waited.

"I shouldn't have insulted your farm," he offered after a bit. "This is a great home. If I had grown up here, I wouldn't be what I am."

"Problems can sprout up anywhere, Colton," she answered, twisting a piece of hay in her fingers. "In the city or on the plains. Anywhere there is land, water, and sunlight."

He nodded. It was true.

But Los Angeles breeds more than its fair share of

poor decision makers...

"So, can we be friends?" Haven asked, changing the subject, pulling him from his thoughts.

Colton looked at her face closely. Her face was weary though her features had yet to age in any meaningful way. She looked tired. Much too tired for someone so young.

Tired of this tricky dance we dance as humans.

He smiled at his lingering melancholy.

"What?"

"Nothing."

She looked at him.

"Yes," he answered, returning to her earlier question. "We can be friends."

And he meant it. He would have liked a friend. More than anything else at that moment, in fact. A friend would have suited Colton just fine.

Chapter Nine

Colton decided to call Moira before she could call him. Leaning forward on his bunk, he waited for her to pick up.

Come on. Come on.

He wanted to get this call over with. Moira would have had time to stew about what had happened, or almost happened rather, with Haven. The earlier lecture was only part one. This phone call would include part two. And perhaps three, four, and five.

"Hey," he said when the ringing stopped.

"Well, hello, Mr. Grey," she responded icily. "It's nice to hear from you. I've informed Jagter of recent events. He's happy that you've called. Aren't you, Jagter?" Colton's publicist cooed as though the famed San Diego lion was seated next to her, enjoying her fingernails scratching at the underside of his chin.

"I told you I'm sorry," he said, wanting to get straight to the point. "I really am. I never meant for anything to happen."

"That's sort of the problem, isn't it? You never mean for any of the things you do to happen."

"Look, I promise. It won't happen again. I wasn't kidding around earlier."

"She's like a sister to me, Colton," Moira reiterated. "That means hands off."

"I know. I do. I really do."

"I've had all afternoon to think about the potential ramifications of you being there, things I didn't think about enough prior to taking you to the farm, and I will not tolerate a single one of them happening."

"I understand."

"Do you?"

"Yes. I do. It was wrong, what I did, forgetting how much you've done for me. But I won't forget again."

"She's doing things for you as well. You have to think about not betraying her trust either."

"I know. I just...I'm not used to people being nice to me. Haven is so nice, so genuine. I got...I wasn't trying to use her. She said something nice to me, and my heart just sort of swelled."

They both did their best to ignore his use of the word *heart* and the word *swell*.

After a bit, during which time each searched for words that weren't right, Moira's voice broke the silence hanging between them.

"Look," she said matter-of-factly. "I understand how cold this industry can be. I get that true kindness can be more alluring than anything else on this planet. But that girl's been through more than anyone deserves to go through. And in only seventeen, almost eighteen, years."

"I know," he responded succinctly. "That's kind of why I was calling."

"Oh?" Moira seemed surprised that Colton knew anything about her cousin's past.

"Yeah. I, uh, I wanted to know what I should get her for her birthday."

"Colton," Moira rebuked, shaking her head. "Have

you heard nothing that I've said?"

"Seriously," he continued, ignoring her. "What would she like?"

"Boundaries, Colton."

"I promise," he stated. "My hands are in the air. Literally. You're now on speaker. I come in peace. I just want to do something nice for her. Something that a friend would do. Not a boyfriend. Will you help me?"

Moira hesitated before admitting, "She's not into material things."

"I gathered. She wears the same five shirts over and over. I haven't bothered to count her jeans."

The venom was back in Moira's voice. "You should know nothing about her jeans, Colton." His publicist's protectiveness of her cousin would have been cute on anybody else. Except Moira had made a name for herself by making sure her bite was far worse than her bark.

"Remember where my hands are, Moira," he reminded. "In the air. Away from any figurative weapons I might own."

"I'm listening."

"It's just…I think she is having money troubles, am I right?"

"I think you shouldn't say anything about that."

"I wasn't planning on saying anything," he assured. "But maybe there is something I can do. I still have a good amount of cash left."

"And a rather steep mortgage and a few other sizable expenses."

"I know that what I have won't last forever. But I'm on the straight and narrow now. I'll have a big payday soon. The kind that will help set me up for life if I put the majority of it away like you always tell me to do."

"Yes."

"So, I was thinking, a few thousand dollars wouldn't be missed if—"

"A few thousand dollars? Colton, she will kill you. And she will kill me for participating in this conversation. People don't just give each other a few thousand dollars in Idaho."

"Surely, in Idaho, someone has given someone else a few thousand dollars," Colton disagreed.

"You know what I mean," Moira said.

"Yes. I do. But I want you to help me anyway."

"This is a bad idea."

She was right. It probably was. But it was the best bad idea Colton had had in a long time. It might even have had a sort of happy ending attached to it. The majority of Colton's bad ideas definitely had not had that going for them. Not even a little bit.

Having been aware of the importance of saying the right thing at just the right time, Colton decided to pull out the most potent verbal ammunition available to him at the moment.

"I didn't want to resort to this," he said. "But if you don't offer a good suggestion, I am putting my money into potato seeds. Lots and lots of potato seeds. Because that's what people grow in Idaho."

"Fine," Moira conceded, amusement and irritation present in her tone in equal measure. "I'll help. But if she gets mad, this is all your fault."

"I understand."

"I had nothing to do with this. You got me?"

"Gotcha."

"And no accepting a thank-you hug if she isn't mad. You can't do that."

"Agreed."

"In fact, maybe you should spend the money on a bubble that you can live in while you are there."

"John Travolta already played that part," Colton pointed out.

"Not as well as you could," Moira volleyed, unwilling to let him win every point in this tennis match of a conversation.

"Blasphemy," Colton responded in a purposefully overemphatic voice. "John Travolta is a legend. You better recognize."

"Don't do that," she demanded. "Don't tell me to recognize. I think I just threw up in my mouth a little."

"After everything I have done, everything you have seen, hearing the word *recognize* is what makes you truly ill?"

"To each their own," she stated.

"Good parry, dear publicist. Good parry. Now, can you help me pick out a present for Haven or what?"

"Or what."

"Potato seeds, Moira. Lots and lots of potato seeds."

"Okay, fine. Give me a second. I just need to pull out my copy of *Tractor Supply*."

"Moira," he growled slightly.

"What? That's what Idahoans are into."

"I'm serious. I need your help."

"And I'm serious. She needs at least a dozen of the things in here."

"Okay," he stammered, a little unsure of what he'd gotten himself into.

"I call dibs on the automatic feeding system. And the mechanized water trough that goes with it. The cows are going to love me."

"What do you think…"

"Jagter says he's going to pick up the digital hay tester."

"Jagter? I thought you had accepted my apology."

"I have. Jagter is still on the fence. He isn't sure you mean it."

"This is going to be a long conversation, isn't it? Longer than necessary?"

"Perhaps," Moira admitted. "It might teach you to follow my orders the first time around. And to answer the phone when I call."

Colton sighed and resigned himself to standing right where he was until his publicist was finished serving up her dish of revenge. Only then would she give him the help he needed.

Chapter Ten

After talking with Moira and discussing all of what a farm girl might want, including new roofs for the chicken coops, Colton had decided that paying off a few of Haven's bills was the best course of action.

It had taken a bit of cajoling to get Moira to use her notorious digging talents to unearth the most pressing of Haven's debts, still it had been worth it. Just the thought of doing anything to make the chickens' lives even a smidgen more comfortable had made him sick.

Now, twenty thousand dollars later as far as Moira was concerned, and a hundred thousand dollars later in reality, Haven's bills were up-to-date.

Colton rationalized this expense. He had spent more on alcohol, drugs, and rehab this year alone. He didn't see a problem with helping out a friend who was saddled with real-life problems, ones not of her own making.

He glanced at the card he had for her. Locked away inside the envelope was a set of receipts showing, as of today, her accounts were current. On the card itself was a note that read:

Haven,

Happy 18th Birthday! Wishing you more than one type of freedom.

Colton

He had started to put "Love, Colton" and thought

better of it. He had been forced to admit words like *love* were used differently in Idaho. They weren't thrown around like they were in Los Angeles.

Plus, the ever-present threat of Jagter, the world's most publicist-friendly lion, was always a speck on the horizon.

Yet, *sincerely* had seemed too generic. Not the kind of word a soberee wrote to a soberer necessarily. So Colton it was. Just Colton. His name was enough for most people. Hopefully, it would turn out to be enough for Haven.

Colton wiped the sweat from his hands. He shouldn't be, but he was nervous. He hadn't done anything like this for somebody before. He had spoiled Anna. Sure. But she could have just as easily spoiled herself. His gifts were tinsel on an already ornately decorated tree.

The gift Colton was giving Haven was meant to be life-changing. More than just show. A true gesture.

"Hey," Haven called as he approached. "What ya got there?"

She was seated at the picnic table at which they had been taking their coffee on occasion. As he sat down, she pushed a steaming cup over to him.

He set the birthday card down in front of her.

"For me?"

He nodded.

She smiled. Gingerly, she separated the flap of the envelope from its body. The pale pink seal gave way under her fingertips.

Time moved slowly as he watched her slide the card out and open it, the receipts inside fluttering to the table. Colton couldn't help it. His heart began to thump.

His nervousness had reached a whole new level.

Haven's eyes jumped over the funny picture of a saddled horse doing a western jig to the words he had scrawled only a short while ago.

Her eyebrows came together in a furrow. She glanced at Colton, then the card again before turning her attention to the receipts. She opened first one, then another, then another. As she did so, her features moved from confusion to shock to understanding to fury.

There was not a single sign of happiness or appreciation in sight. Not even a shred of relief.

"You had no right, Colton. No right," she started.

Hugs would not be forthcoming. About that Moira could be certain.

Rising from the picnic bench at which they were seated, Haven set herself to pacing. "This is wrong."

He shook his head. He couldn't help it. As far as he was concerned, this was the rightest thing he had ever done.

"This is wrong, Colton. Can't you see that? How could you do this?"

His heart was thumping louder in his chest now. He didn't know what to say. "I was trying to help…"

"You can't just pry into other people's affairs." Haven halted. She was facing away from him.

"I wasn't trying to pry," he finally responded, getting up from the picnic bench.

She didn't answer.

Against his better judgment and with Moira's voice in his head screaming for him to stay the hell back, Colton closed the distance between them. Then, with gentle hands, he turned her around. "I was trying to make things better for you."

Haven's lower lip quivered. Her eyes remained downcast. She was fighting tears. He realized then that he had never seen her cry.

It was a strange sight to say the least.

"I'm sorry," he said, ashamed that he was the cause of her suffering.

She nodded her head, unable to turn her gaze up to him.

"I'll—" he started to promise.

"There's nothing you can do," she said, fighting the moisture swelling in her eyes. "Creditors won't give you the money back."

"It's okay," he reassured.

"It's not okay," she countered, more in control now, sight still focused intently on the ground. "I can never repay you."

"You've done more for me than anyone," he said, tipping her face up, willing her to understand.

"That's not true."

"It is. You've seen me as a person. Not a hero, not a villain. You've accepted me, the bad and the good. You've been a friend."

"Friends don't pay each other for their services."

"That's not payment, Haven. That's help. Exactly what you've given me."

Haven looked him in the eye, listening intently.

"You're eighteen, Haven. Four years younger than me. And far more burdened than I have ever been. I created my problems. I suspect that you've inherited yours."

"Yes," she eventually breathed.

He had to hold himself back from further proving his point. Instead, he let her stare off into the distance like he so often did when he was collecting his thoughts. He felt more vulnerable than he had in a long time. For whatever reason, he couldn't stand the thought of Haven being mad at him. Not for his kindness. Not when he'd been trying to help.

When he could take the quiet no longer, he asked, "Can you forgive me?"

She took a deep breath, her pride threatening to upset the peace that he was negotiating. A few more ragged exhalations and one long sigh later, she responded, "On one condition."

"What's that?" The eagerness to say yes was apparent in his voice.

"Tomorrow, we go riding."

Colton didn't quite follow. "I'm not saying no. But why?"

"Because I promised to force you to," she answered, a hopefulness beneath her sadness. "And I always make good on my promises."

"Tomorrow, then," he agreed. "We go riding."

Haven smiled weakly, then turned to leave.

Colton watched her go.

Once Haven returned to her house and the mother that had never so much as introduced herself, the mother whose mental health condition had contributed to a portion of the bills he had recently paid off, Colton returned to his bunk and lay on his cot.

Arms behind his head, he took a deep breath.

"Haven," he whispered.

All of a sudden, there was more meaning in that one word than in any he had ever uttered.

"Haven," he said again, feeling the weight of her name on his tongue.

Chapter Eleven

"Your seat's pretty good," Haven complimented from atop Cicero.

They were riding in a field full of long grass that would be harvested and turned into some kind of hay when the time was right.

"We call it something else in LA," Colton responded.

"Not your rear," she amended. "The way you follow your horse's stride. Your seat."

He ignored her correction.

"It's always something physical with you. First, you spray me down in your own private wet T-shirt contest. Then you almost kiss me."

"Colton."

"I'm kidding. I'm kidding," he said, enjoying the feeling of the breeze on his face. "I think I'm still high from the gallop we just took." Immediately, he regretted his choice of words. "You know what I mean," he added quickly.

"I know," she said in a serious tone. A silence spread between them until she broke it. "There is nothing wrong with feeling good, you know?"

"I know," he said.

"It's just the way that you get there that can be the problem. And the steep fall afterwards."

"I understand, Haven. Trust me, I do." He was

more frustrated than he should be. But having someone four years his junior tell him about life, and seem to be so much better at living than he was, was a bit of a wake-up call, one that left him feeling slightly less than stellar about himself.

When he sighed, after a stretch of silence, Haven decided to say something else. "I'm sorry," she said. "I know that you know. I just didn't know what else to say."

He didn't respond. Not because he was mad any longer, but because his mind had drifted to the run they had just taken with their mounts. The way Haven's hair had flown out behind her, straight and the perfect mixture of red and brown. Russet in the sunlight, chocolate when wet, her hair color was the shade he liked best.

And Colton knew what that meant. His mind was definitely crossing the boundary between friendship and something else. With each day that passed, he thought about her more and more.

This was their fifth ride together. The first had been a disaster. Riding a horse was not like riding a bike. Far from it, as it had turned out. Changing gears was not a matter of pressing a lever and pumping your foot harder. No. When riding a horse, another brain lay between the rider's decision and the change he sought. Or she sought, when the rider was a girl.

Haven might have been all cool and collected from the beginning of their rides. But Colton had required more than a few attempts at going from a walk to a trot and from a trot to a canter. Eventually, he had reached enough comfort with the process to attempt a gallop. His life in his horse's hands, he'd done his best to keep up with Haven.

Something he'd been doing for some time.

Which was exactly what had been worrying Moira. Had her worried still. The multitude of promises he had made on every phone call since Haven's birthday, when he said he felt nothing beyond friendship for his publicist's cousin, had done nothing to calm Moira's worries. Nor had it stemmed the litany of her increasingly creative threats of bodily harm.

She hadn't even noticed that he had stopped cracking sexual jokes, a feat for someone like him. He had prided himself on his dirty humor. Sexual jokes were his comedic mainstay. Now, he was left trying to find something funny in the more innocent aspects of life, not exactly familiar territory.

During their last phone call, Moira had slowly transitioned off the topic of Haven and onto the topic of his new movie. He was one month and one week sober. The suits behind the soon-to-be blockbuster were impressed with his accomplishment.

Plus, there had been no further bad publicity. Since the incident with the reporter uncovering his old phone number, no one else had called him on his secure cell.

As a precaution, Moira continued to mail out new phones with new numbers every week, just in case, which was expensive, but not nearly as costly as a negative story in the press would have ended up being.

"Colton."

"Yes," he responded, waking from his haze.

"You want to try jumping?" Haven asked.

"As in jacks? Maybe. I do need to tone up a bit."

"Not jacks. Horses."

"I don't think I can leap a tall horse in a single

bound." He paused for emphasis. "Besides, Ol' Faithful here would not like that. She's a gentle creature, unused to the ways of crazy and obnoxious humans."

"Actually, she's who we put all of our most obnoxious visitors on." Haven smirked at him, waiting for his response.

"But do you put the crazies on her?" he countered. "I don't think so."

"You're our first crazy." The last word barely left Haven's lips.

Instantly, Colton regretted making the joke. The other day, when Mrs. Morrow had answered the door, just as he was arriving at the main house to ask Haven a question, she had gripped his arm firmly and said thank you, with eyes lit up by whatever agony kept her locked up inside of her house all day.

Haven had slipped past her mom as quickly as she could, pushing Colton away from the door and down the porch. She had then proceeded to avoid Colton's gaze the entire time she had answered his questions.

His heart had beat quickly. He'd wanted to hug her, tell her everything was going to be okay. But that was never a guarantee anyone could keep. He knew that. No matter how beautiful the surface, there were always currents churning erratically underneath.

It had taken a day for Haven to be able to resume her regular eye contact with him. Another twenty-four hours for her to allow one of her carefree smiles to grace her face unguarded.

Since he'd paid off her debts, she'd been gentler, not just with him, but with their work. The haste that was driving her to move from task to task without so much as a breath in between had slowed. She had still been keeping them plenty busy. But since she'd accepted his help, she allowed herself a moment here and there to soak up her surroundings.

Colton supposed a weight had been lifted off her shoulders, albeit temporarily. Being without was one thing. Having everything that you loved taken away from you bit by bit was quite another.

Especially when you were eighteen.

Eighteen.

Haven seemed older to Colton, older than he was. Not because of the way she looked. She looked young. But because of her unique brand of wisdom.

Looking back at her, seeing her lost in her thoughts, he had the sudden urge to do anything to make her happy, which was why he agreed to the worst idea she had proposed since he had arrived at her place weeks ago.

"Okay," he called back.

"Okay what?" she asked, forgetting what she'd suggested.

"Okay. We can jump our horses."

She smiled.

"Just let me say a few prayers first. Then dismount. Get a running start. After that, I will jump whatever horse you ask me to."

"Always the comedian," she said.

"My critics would disagree with you," he called back, thrilled that he had been able to amuse her. Just this once.

Chapter Twelve

Colton walked bowlegged back into the barn. As it turned out, jumping a horse hurt. Badly. Especially if you landed incorrectly in the saddle, which he had done twice, or if you fell off, which he had done once.

He caught Haven suppressing a laugh. He knew he looked a fright. There were mud smears on his face and what he could only guess were manure stains on his pants. When they'd led their horses by the chicken barn, he'd sworn he could hear the chickens laughing at him.

Damn evil beasts, he thought.

Colton couldn't wait to take a quick shower and go to sleep. He was exhausted. He felt like he did after a hard day of stunts, except he didn't have an earnings bonus to look forward to after all of his hard work. Just an uncomfortable bunk bed and the darkness of the night's sky.

Colton and Haven washed their horses, patted them dry with towels that wicked away moisture like he had never seen, and rubbed some liniment on their legs for good measure. He followed her lead because that was what he had done every day since his arrival on the farm. She was the expert here. He the apprentice. Working toward a small sense of accomplishment before he returned to the world whose patterns and expectation had driven him here in the first place.

"I was thinking," he said as the idea struck him, "that we should go to town sometime soon."

"Do you think that's such a good idea?" Haven responded.

"Of course. Why not? Don't you? You haven't been off the farm in ages."

"I rarely leave."

"But surely, you want to celebrate your graduation from high school."

"It's not like I graduated two years ahead of schedule like you."

"I wasn't running a farm."

"But you were making movies."

"That's true. But my grades weren't that great."

"Are you playing the humble hero all of a sudden? It's not like you to turn down a chance to brag."

"Ha ha," he responded, knowing she was speaking the truth more than she knew. When she didn't respond, he asked again, "Seriously. Can we go out for a day?"

"First, you have to tell me why you want to leave."

"I am doing well here. I think I should see if I can leave isolation and remain sober."

"You think you can handle it?"

"With you as my sober coach? Of course. You'd kill anybody who offered me so much as extra cream in my coffee."

She smiled. "It would be nice to get away," she admitted. "The crew that harvests the hay is coming out in a few days. We can go then. I trust the guy in charge. He'll assign a couple of his guys to feed the cows and horses while we are gone."

"Great."

"Where do you want to go?"

"Where is the nearest movie theater?"

"Seriously. You want to take me to see one of your movies?"

"You need to read the paper more. Or better yet, use the Internet for something other than crop research and looking up the latest price for beef. If you did, you would know that I don't have any movies out right now."

"Then why do you want to go to the theater?"

"I can't stand the idea of you not liking movies. There has to be something out now that can change your mind."

"I'm not so sure…"

"Seriously, Haven. It would be good for both of us to get out. If you don't want to see a movie, we don't have to. But I am certain that the theaters in your neck of the woods don't sell alcohol. So, I won't have to watch you watching me to see if my eyes glance at the wine list at a fancy restaurant."

She looked like he'd slapped her. "I'm not trying to…"

"I know," he said. "I'm sorry."

After a bit, he added, "I just want to know that I can do it. That my success isn't due to total isolation, but to a change within me. That's all."

"Okay," she said. "We'll go. I promise."

Chapter Thirteen

The day that Colton and Haven were supposed to leave on their trip had come. Rather than heading out as soon as she could, Haven got caught up in overseeing the harvest.

At first, Colton was disappointed. She'd promised after all. Soon after, his disappointment turned to anger. Then his anger to rage. Until, finally, his rage transformed itself into an uncontrollable urge to get as far away from her and this farm as he could.

In seconds, he was in her truck, turning the key that she always left hanging in the ignition, driving down the highway away from everything he'd recently come to know. It was only when he was less than forty miles away from his destination that his phone rang.

He toyed with the idea of not answering it before giving in to his better instincts. "Colton here," he offered nonchalantly.

"Colton, where are you?" Haven's voice trembled with worry.

"I'm in your truck," he answered coolly, aiming for the high ground in this conversation.

"I guessed that. But where are you going?"

"I am going exactly where we planned to go."

"You shouldn't have left…"

"It was clear you weren't going to break away. So, I am making the journey myself."

"Colton, we could have always gone another day."

"We agreed to today." His tone was bitter, more so than he expected. His high ground was slipping away. Swiftly.

"I'm sorry, Colton. I really wanted to go. I…I'm…I guess I'm still worried about the future of the farm."

With each word she uttered, he felt guilty. And with each pang of guilt, his frustration increased. The calm that the open road had brought him was dissipating.

"Colton, are you there?"

"Yes," he answered.

"Are you mad at me?"

Silence greeted her.

"Colton, I get it. I messed up. That doesn't mean…"

"Doesn't mean what, Haven? Just say it."

"Doesn't mean you should use."

He knew it. She thought he had set out to use. Nothing else.

"This trip isn't about using," he countered. "It's about the opposite. It's about showing myself that I don't have to use, that I can get through a day away from Moira's carefully constructed lockdown without snorting or swigging away."

"You don't have anyone with you."

"And whose fault is that?" He knew he was going too far. But he couldn't stop himself.

"Colton, you chose to drive off without me. I am not responsible for that."

She was right.

"What's really the problem?" she asked.

He sighed. How could he explain? "This day wasn't just about me," he reticently admitted.

It was her turn to be silent.

With nothing left to say and nothing coming from her to build upon, Colton said, "I have to go."

"I'm sorry," Haven offered.

"Not enough," he mumbled before hanging up the phone.

She called again a short time later and left a voicemail. "Colton, it's me. Please come home soon."

The vulnerability in her voice was enough to break him, to tear a chunk out of his inner workings. To whittle him down to nothing but regret and awareness of his stubborn selfishness.

Nevertheless, he gripped the steering wheel. He would make it to the town they had chosen. And he would show himself and her that he could move about the world without drinking or doing drugs.

Chapter Fourteen

Colton woke up to the bright sun in his face.

He looked around the truck. In the corner was a bottle. Thankfully, it was full, the seal still intact. He searched his pockets for baggies. There were none to be found.

He counted the money in his wallet. He was only missing thirty dollars, enough for the bottle of liquor that stared him down and the food once housed in cellophane wrappers now strewn about his feet.

For some reason, he'd crashed hard the evening before. He couldn't remember sleeping that well since he had accidentally taken a downer when he had meant to take an upper and was forced to catnap at Rebound Fling #1's apartment. Her entire bed had been covered in goose down. From mattress topper to pillows to comforter, the bed had been heaven.

Unfortunately, the waking-up process had not been so blissful. As soon as the girl had realized that the fifteen minutes of heaven she'd shared with him were the only fifteen minutes she would ever get, she'd kicked him out, keeping his shoes as a souvenir.

Understandably, the walk home had been rough, both figuratively and literally.

His journey had ended with another one of Moira's lectures, this one a half hour in length and aimed at getting him to stop his downward spiral. When she could tell that he had soaked up all of what he could or would from her words, she'd sent him to take a shower and shave the three-day-old stubble from his face.

In all fairness, he'd ensured that she would read him the riot act. He'd called her from a pay phone after the bottoms of his feet had started to ribbon.

"A beard won't do on a mug like yours," Moira had stage whispered when sending him off to shave, doing her best to impersonate a secretary in a gangster flick from the 1950s.

The stubble he had had then was not all that different from the stubble he had now.

The prickly feeling of partially grown-out hairs brought him back to the present. He fought the urge to scratch the thick whiskers along his jawline as he forced himself to undertake movement. He didn't think it wise to wait around to be recognized.

A day's worth of stubbly growth would not a disguise make.

Colton started Haven's truck, then pulled out of the parking lot of a miniature golf course.

Nothing odd about spending the night next to pint-sized putting greens, he thought. *Nothing odd at all.*

A mile or so down the road, he pulled into a gas station so he could use the restroom and fill up the truck. Once he'd filled the tank and disposed of the full bottle of liquor by tossing it in the trash can between pumps three and four, he climbed back in the truck and broke the seal on the water he'd just purchased. It wasn't his favorite libation. But it didn't bring with it the consequences of the former either.

"Ahhhh," he exhaled in perfect commercial falsetto.

Shortly thereafter, as he was pulling out of town, his cell phone rang. It barely had any juice left. But he answered anyway.

"Colton, you need to get back to Haven's."

"I know."

"No. You don't. Her mother's sick. She's had another attack…"

"What's wrong?" he asked.

"I don't know exactly. But judging by Haven's voice, it's bad."

Colton said his good-byes and pressed the gas pedal before Moira could get another word in edgewise.

Of course, he thought. *She wasn't just worried about leaving the farm. She was worried about leaving others alone on the farm.*

He'd been so stupid.

The 111 miles separating him from Haven couldn't fly by fast enough. He prayed that the cops between him and the girl he seemed to disappoint around every corner were busy with something else. Or uninterested in his speed. It couldn't be profitable to station a police officer in every one-stop-sign town between him and Haven.

Then again, how else might they earn their revenue?

A little less than two hours after the phone call from Moira, Colton and his lead foot arrived at Haven's farm. The truck was barely in park before he was out of the driver's side door, running toward the main house. His pulse pounding in his ears, his breath a herd of wild horses urging him faster across the mini-plain.

Haven looked lost, standing on the porch, clutching herself with lonely arms. She gazed into the distance, silent and immutable. The front door to the main house was open. The porch and yard were silent as any grave. There were no health workers or first responders milling about. They must have taken her mom away.

Colton leapt up the stairs to the porch in one bound. He was by her side in less than a second after that. As soon as he was close enough, Haven collapsed into him.

"She's in the hospital again," she confessed, talking into his chest.

"I know," he said, pulling her further into him.

"She thought I was trying to hurt her."

He couldn't imagine any person thinking Haven was capable of hurting a single soul.

"She tried to choke me."

At that, Colton separated himself from Haven, guiding her far enough back that he could get a good look at her.

Bruises the size of a woman's fingertips formed a necklace on her soft, white skin.

"I tried so hard to keep her out of the hospital," she said, her voice cracking.

"I know you did," he reassured, pulling her into him once more. "When she's better, she'll know you did, too."

Except she might not. Not all people recovered from their breaks. Haven's mother certainly hadn't. Not yet. Colton berated himself for making a promise he couldn't keep, one that had nothing to do with him.

Then he transitioned to berating himself for spending his night sulking, flirting with the idea of throwing away everything he'd ever earned down the drain while Haven had been forced to try to protect herself from the woman she loved most.

After a few buckets of tears and a hundred whispered *shh*s later, Haven looked up at him. "I can't do this anymore," she said. "It's not working."

He didn't know what to say in return.

"Why does it have to be so hard?" she asked a moment later, hiccups interrupting her syllables.

Again, Colton was without wisdom.

Being unable to do what he'd been doing was territory that Colton was more than familiar with. As was recognizing that a chosen path was hard. But he hadn't found any solutions to either problem. Other than spending time with Haven, he had yet to figure out a way to push himself past what he could tolerate.

So, instead of trying to offer up an answer, he allowed her to cry some more.

As she did, Colton willed Haven to absorb whatever strength he had left. She was the most important person in the world to him right now, perhaps ever.

That, he knew, was love. Love like he had never felt before. Love that Moira would hate him for. And love that he wasn't sure he could be worthy of, no matter how hard he tried.

The problem was he couldn't order himself to stop feeling it.

If he could, he'd have had an answer for the girl in his arms, and they would have both been able to walk away from the things that had hurt them the most and that had made them into the people they had become.

Chapter Fifteen

Once Haven had cried herself into a sleepy silence, she raised her eyes to meet Colton's. The jolt that ran through his chest in response was almost too much to take.

As soon as he was able to, he disentangled himself from her. He was not the person she should look at like that. Not now. Not ever.

"Colton, where are you going?"

"To take care of the horses. They need to be turned out, right?"

She nodded her head and wiped at her eyes while he jogged away from her.

Moira called him just after he had released Cicero into a nearby field.

"Hello," he said.

"Is she okay?"

Colton plugged his phone into an outlet in the tack room. There was a negligible amount of battery power left.

"Yes," he whispered.

"Why are you whispering?"

"I don't know where she is right now, and I don't want her to hear us talking."

"Where are you?"

"In the tack room of the barn so my phone can charge."

"I see."

There was silence between them for a while. Then, Colton said, "Moira, I didn't drink or use," just as she was asking, "So, how bad was the relapse?"

She sighed, taking in what he'd said. "Does Haven know?"

"No. I haven't had the chance to tell her. She was too upset. All I could do was hold her. My bad-boy ways are the last thing on her mind right now."

"You know you're not a bad person." Moira softened.

"If it looks like a duck and walks like a duck…"

"My word, you have been on that farm for too long."

He chuckled at that.

"Did the trip help out?"

Yes and no, he wanted to say. Instead, he offered a sigh of his own.

"It's happened, hasn't it?"

"Moira, I just got through telling you that I didn't drink…"

"Not that, Colton. You've fallen for Haven, haven't you?"

"No."

But his answer was too quick, too strong. So, now, Moira really did know and no longer suspected.

After a time, she said, "I can't say I am happy about this…"

"Tell me about it," he added, because he wasn't happy about it either.

Haven was too good for him. But his stupid heart wouldn't listen to reason.

"Does she know?"

"No. No, of course not. She deserves far better than me."

Again, Moira took her time with her words. "The old you wasn't good enough for her, Colton. That I'll concede. But the new you, maybe…" Every word appeared to cause her strain.

"Why are you saying this?"

"Because you rushed back to be with her. Because you held her while she cried."

"I am less than two months sober."

"And those sober months have been spent with her."

Colton was in shock. Moira, his publicist, the woman who knew every single one of his bad exploits, was practically giving him the green light to pursue her cousin. After having threatened to feed him to the first wild beast she could think of if he so much as considered having an impure thought about her cousin, she was now singing a different tune.

"Moira, I'm not going to. I can't," he said, just as Haven asked, "You can't what?"

Colton hung up the phone almost as efficiently as he ignored her question.

"You can't what?" Haven repeated.

"Nothing," he muttered, staring at his hands. "Moira was just asking me if I could leave a couple weeks early to start shooting the movie. I told her that I need more time. To devote to my sobriety."

"You're lying," Haven said.

It was a simple fact. He was lying. But to hear her call him out on it was unsettling. He looked around the barn, at the stall doors, up at the rafters, anywhere but in Haven's eyes.

"Colton?"

His name. From her lips. His heart beat more quickly. "Yes," he finally answered.

"Tell me one thing."

"No."

"No, you won't tell me?"

"No. I didn't use."

"I know."

"You know?"

"Yes."

"How?"

"I could see it in your eyes."

"But I was gone all night."

"Because I had upset you," she replied, taking a step closer.

"It wasn't you," he confessed, taking a small step of his own back.

"Wasn't it?" she asked, cocking her head, both at his response and at his attempt to keep his distance.

He didn't answer. This was a dangerous game she was playing. He had self-control. He'd been working on that on a near-constant basis recently. But with her looking at him the way she was, he wasn't sure how long he could keep himself in check.

"What is your question if it isn't about my drinking?"

"Were you and Moira talking about me?"

He froze. Then, when he saw she wasn't planning on moving the conversation forward until he answered, he nodded his head reluctantly.

"Did she call you to tell you about my mom?"

"Yes."

"Is that why you rushed home? To be with me?"

"Yes."

Her voice suddenly went husky when she said his name. "Colton."

Just his name was enough. He wanted, no, he needed to get himself out of this predicament. "Haven, please…" He tried because he couldn't move. Not yet.

"What?" she asked innocently.

"You're eighteen," he reminded.

"I'm aware of my age," she said, again in a voice he didn't recognize.

What was happening was wrong. All wrong. It wasn't Haven.

Still, he was responding just the same.

"I can't give you what you want," he breathed. It was all he had. All he could think of at the present moment.

"How could you know what I want," she challenged, her body moving in a way he hadn't seen.

Because I've had thousands of women throw themselves at me like you are doing now, he thought to himself.

"Colton?" Her voice was her own again, if just for a second.

It was enough to help him speak, to help him think, to help him do anything other than let the scene before him play out any further. "I can't do this," he said, moving past her and walking back to his bunk.

Her footsteps followed him.

After he entered his sleeping quarters, the door failed to close behind him. He turned around to see her standing in the doorway. A breeze whipped her hair about. Her face was still blotchy from crying, but she was as beautiful to him as she had ever been.

"Don't do this," he begged.

"Do what?" she said, taking a step closer.

"Haven, I'm serious. I'm not what you need right now."

Her hands began working one of her buttons loose.

"Haven, stop."

The force with which he commanded her to cease pursuing him shocked her out of her stupor. "Colton, I…"

Her heart was breaking once more. That he could see. But he couldn't hold her now. She had to leave. If she didn't, he would do something he couldn't take back, something he would regret for the rest of his life.

"Haven, you have to go. Now."

Her face flinched.

"I said now," he repeated, his voice raised more than before.

She nodded her head, slowly backed out of the doorway, then ran away from him.

Colton could do nothing except pace the floor of his bunk. He was furious. With himself. With her. With himself some more. Her mother was in a hospital somewhere, and he'd just yelled at her. He was a monster.

And why couldn't she see that he was only trying to protect her? His rejection didn't result from a lack of attraction. His rejection was based on moral principle.

A little while later, just as he was thinking about performing an amateur lobotomy on himself so he could separate his consciousness from the thoughts that haunted him, his phone rang. He'd thrown it in his pocket, charger still intact when he'd escaped from the barn. He answered it, yanking out the charger once it was free from his pocket and throwing it on his bed.

"This is Colton."

"What did you do?" Moira asked.

"Nothing. I swear. I didn't do anything."

"She called me and told me to come get you."

Colton shoved his hand into his hair. Haven wanted him to leave. What had he thought would happen? That things would go back to the way they were before everything happened?

"You swear you didn't do anything?"

"I didn't."

"I don't understand then…"

He couldn't tell Moira her cousin had thrown herself at him and, because he hadn't taken her up on her offer, she wanted him to leave. To divulge such private information seemed like a transgression somehow. No matter how close she and her cousin were, Haven deserved to keep that to herself. So, he remained silent.

"Fine. I'll be there the day after tomorrow," Moira signed off. "Keep your distance until then."

Once it was dark, Colton went for a walk. At first, his steps were aimless. But it wasn't long until he found himself back in the barn.

Haven must have brought the horses back in because Ol' Faithful was munching away on the hay in the right-hand corner of her stall. When she saw him, she paused her chewing and walked over to allow him to scratch behind her ears.

"I screwed up," he told the horse, suddenly aware that he was hungry, too.

Ol' Faithful sneezed all over him.

"That's what she said." He chuckled, even though

it wasn't at all funny.

He'd thought he had a month to make his peace with leaving Haven and all they'd shared behind. Now, he had less than forty-eight hours.

He couldn't believe how things had ended up. He'd always thought, if she kicked him out, it would be because he had used—either alcohol or her. But he'd done neither. He'd been as good as he had ever been. And this was what his good behavior had earned him.

Colton walked into the tack room refrigerator and grabbed a few carrots. One, he took a large bite out of. The other, he offered to Ol' Faithful as a treat.

"A little stale," he said. But at least they weren't slimy. Slimy carrots, like slimy people, were the worst.

Chapter Sixteen

The next day, Colton did as he was told. He kept his distance.

Outside of his bunk, he found a few provisions. One, a mug of coffee with a paper towel over it. The other, a sandwich in a plastic baggie. The salami was still cold from the refrigerator. So, it hadn't been on the porch long.

Colton wolfed down the food and headed out to the barn. He saw Haven going into one of the industrial-sized chicken coops, which made it clear she was avoiding him, too. There was no way he would follow her in there.

After feeding and watering the horses, he saddled Ol' Faithful and rode out to check the fences. He'd done little more than nail a board or two back in place on his rounds. Still, it was more than he'd ever done before.

Colton stayed out of the pasture where the bull resided. That beast looked fit to kill on a constant basis.

The fields full of hay only days ago had been shorn. The grass sat, drying in the sun. He imagined the men would be back out soon to bale it. Haven had mentioned that she planned to store some and sell the rest, the best of her supply, to nearby farms and feed stores.

Before long, Colton urged Ol' Faithful into a

canter. There was nothing else to do. He and Haven had already fixed everything that needed to be fixed.

Once he was a good distance away from the animals closest to him, he sent Ol' Faithful into a gallop. She didn't so much as balk at his command. Instead, she raced as fast as she could into the light breeze that worked its way across the land. Colton enjoyed the sensation of the wind on his face. He leaned into it. But he didn't smile.

No matter what he did, the ache that had started when Haven had walked out of his bunk wouldn't stop.

It was infuriating.

A little while later, Colton slowed Ol' Faithful to a walk. He laid the reins on the winded horse's neck and stretched his arms up into the air. He would be sore this evening, but the thrill had been worth it. The gallop had given him a taste of the freedom he longed for, the kind of reprieve that drove a thirst that couldn't be quenched.

Colton had no idea if he was ready to rejoin Hollywood. Without a movie to throw himself into, he'd have too much time on his hands. Which had always been his downfall.

But he couldn't think of that now. Instead, he had to focus. He had to find the words to show Haven he was thankful for how much she had done for him. Whether she was mad at him or just embarrassed, she needed to know he wasn't mad at her. Not anymore.

Any anger he'd felt was fleeting, born of the fact that she'd forced him to protect her by hurting her feelings. He'd never wanted to be in that position. He didn't still. Knowing this, though, did nothing to birth the words he needed to say.

Haven was wounded the instant he turned her

down. The hurt was more than apparent in her eyes. Crisp, clear, true.

If he had to guess, he would say that last night had been the first time she had offered herself to anyone. Her movements were too rehearsed, too unnatural, too much like the idea of what somebody thought was sexy, not what actually was.

Watching her stray from who she was into the vision of a forty-something-year-old B-movie-maker's wet dream had been difficult to say the least. Responding to it in any way, so much worse. It had made him feel like a perversion of nature, more like the person the tabloids painted him out to be than he cared to admit.

At that, Colton shook the image from his head and turned Ol' Faithful back to the barn. By the time he got back, he'd know what to say. He'd have to. Time was running out. It was just that simple.

Chapter Seventeen

Colton dropped Ol' Faithful's bridle onto a hook, then walked out of the barn through the side door. On his way out, he grabbed a broom so he could sweep the porch that surrounded the bunkhouse. It needed a good cleaning. He'd noticed that this morning when he'd grabbed the sandwich Haven had left out for him.

Colton twirled the broom as he walked, giving his hands something to do. As physically demanding as his ride had been, he was still full of energy that had nowhere to go. Once back at the bunkhouse, he set the borrowed broom next to the screen door and headed inside. He needed to check his phone before he did anything else.

Sure enough, Moira had left him several messages.

"Bad news," she said in one voicemail. "There's been a crisis with one of my other clients. Lots of cleanup needed. It's going to be a few days before I can come get you. Don't leave on your own and hang in there."

Another message said, "It may be as long as a week. Sorry. Stay put. I'll let you know when I am coming as soon as I know."

The third was slightly frantic. "Colton, call me when you get this. I need to know that you and Haven are not at each other's throats. I'm a little worried."

Colton sighed, then returned Moira's call. When

she failed to answer, he left his own voicemail. In a mock cheery voice, he assured her no one was dead and murder hadn't been threatened, not even once.

After he was finished, he selected the option to review the voicemail that he had just left. It sounded real enough. Upbeat. Patient. Everything he wasn't feeling at the moment. Satisfied that he had done his part, Colton certified that the message was listener-worthy, then mashed the end button so hard that his thumb stung.

The acting on-screen he could take. The constant expectation that he should be on his mark in real life was a little bit of a problem.

Nonetheless, there were places to go, people to see, and skin to clean. So, he grabbed his towel and headed to the shower. The grime and filth clinging to him had to be removed as soon as possible.

Under the stream of water, he allowed himself to think about Haven. How could she not understand that his intentions had been noble? He'd saved her from making a huge mistake. Shouldn't she be thankful?

Instead, she'd gotten mad and had been keeping herself at a distance ever since. It was clear: She didn't want to see his face. Normally, Colton would have had to at least kiss a girl to get that kind of reaction. Kiss her, then move on to the next girl, and then the next. Not remain gentlemanly and polite.

Well, maybe he hadn't been polite. But he'd been gentlemanly. He hadn't accepted what Haven was offering. That was something.

By the time Colton returned to his sleeping quarters, there was a plate of food outside his door. Something about the foil-covered dish and the plastic-wrapped milk beside it got his ire up.

Quickly, Colton threw on some clothes, grabbed his food, and headed up to Haven's house. Once there, he knocked on the door. Hard.

When there was no answer, he walked in anyway. Haven had on headphones and was bopping her head to music he couldn't hear.

"Excuse me," he called out, setting down his hand-delivered dinner.

She couldn't hear him.

"Excuse me," he said again.

Still nothing.

"Haven."

At her name, she turned around.

Colton had read once that people could hear their own names better than anything else that was said, no matter the amount of background noise. Apparently, that information was true.

Haven lowered her headphones, staring at him in disbelief.

"Moira won't be here tomorrow," he confessed. It seemed the most important piece of information that he had to share at the moment.

"I know," she replied, deadpan. Her tone gave nothing of her feelings away.

"So, we can't avoid each other for days."

"Why not? It's a big farm."

Haven's reply was full of spite. Ever the awful card player, Colton saw her spite and raised her a serving of petulance.

"Well, I don't like my dinner with a side of ants."

The truth was there were no ants in his dinner, not anywhere. He'd checked. How there weren't any, he didn't know. But his plate and glass of milk were both ant-free.

Haven, predictably, called him on his bluff. "The ground around and under the bunkhouse has been treated. Ants won't bother your dinner."

"Flies, then. I don't want a side of flies with my dinner."

Folding was not an option here.

"I put tinfoil on your plate and clear plastic wrap over your glass of milk. I think you're fine." She knew this discussion had nothing to do with insects. And she was making it clear that she had no intention of helping him get where he was trying to go.

"Haven, come on. We have to talk," he finally offered. That was as much of an olive branch as he could fashion at the moment.

Still, she swatted it away. "As I recall, Mr. Grey, the last time that I wanted to talk, you threw me out of your bunk."

It's your bunk, he wanted to say. *All of this is yours.* But he didn't. Because she wouldn't understand what he was saying. Hell, he wasn't even sure what he was saying.

"You know I did the right thing," he finally answered, which was exactly the wrong thing to say. He could tell.

Her face fell. "Please leave," she whispered, looking at her hands.

But he didn't. He couldn't. She had to know. "Haven, come on."

"I said, 'Please leave.' " Her voice was louder now but still nowhere near as loud as usual.

Perhaps it was Haven's apparent vulnerability,

perhaps it was the fear that he would never talk to the girl before him as he once had, but Colton was compelled to confess everything, everything he'd been holding back.

Everything Moira had once warned him he was never allowed to feel let alone share.

"Haven," he started, "I asked you to leave the other day because I didn't want you to go."

She looked up, allowed her gaze to fall on his face rather than to rest on her own hands. She was studying him.

"You were speaking to me in a way you had never spoken to me before, and I liked it. I knew it was wrong, but I liked it. You were speaking to me from a place of pain, yet I was responding. You weren't being yourself. Still, I was tempted."

"Colton, I—"

"No. Please. Let me finish. You were offering me something. Something, I suspect, that you have never offered anybody before. And I couldn't take it. If I had taken it, I would have become exactly what the tabloids have made me out to be. A monster."

"Colton…"

"Haven, you have to know. I wanted you. More than I've wanted anything else in my whole life. More than I've wanted alcohol. More than I've wanted drugs. I wanted you. And the timing wasn't right. The circumstances weren't right. There was no other answer I could give you…You deserved…you still deserve…"

He let his voice trail off. He was fighting back emotions he could not name. He'd laid himself bare.

"Why wasn't it right?" she asked, hesitantly.

"Because you were hurting, Haven. Can't you see?

I didn't want to take advantage."

"I was offering myself to you, Colton, not the other way around."

"I know," he muttered.

"So, you think I am unable to decide what I want? That I don't know myself?"

"I think you were trying to numb the pain."

She looked at him as if to say, *So?*

"If there's one thing I've learned, it's that numbing the pain doesn't work. Not in the long run."

She took a step closer, raising her hand as if to touch him, to comfort him.

"Haven, no. I'm not here for that."

"You don't get to decide what I do."

"You're right. I don't. But I can choose what I'll do. And I won't do this. Not now. Not with you."

She looked wounded. Deeply wounded. She turned her back to him.

I can't win. Nothing I say will make this better.

But he tried anyway. "Haven, please. Listen to what I am saying."

"I heard what you said. You said you won't do this. Not now. Not with me."

"Did you hear the rest?"

"You said you wanted me. But anybody can say that, Colton. Words are just words."

He knew that better than anybody. He'd spoken enough false words for them both.

But the words he'd shared with Haven were his own. They were not a small string in a larger set of lines. Nobody had written him a script. They had come from a place he hadn't allowed to see daylight in a long, long time.

"Haven," he said again, taking a step closer, putting his hand on her shoulder. "I—"

She turned to face him. Her wanting burned brightly. "Please," she whispered.

Colton took her visage in.

Her green eyes were intoxicating. Her lips were luscious and full. Her skin was radiant.

"Don't ask me for this," he whispered back. "I'm begging you."

In response, she leaned up, touched his face, then placed her lips on his.

And just like that, his resolve vanished. He couldn't say no. Not with her mouth on his. Not with the way she tasted. Not with the soft sounds she was making in the back of her throat.

After a few passes of her lips over his, Colton could barely remain upright. So he moved them to lean against the kitchen counter and took over the kissing.

He deepened it. He was losing track of time and space. With each movement of their hungry mouths, Colton was losing all contact with sanity and reason.

Stop this. His brain was screaming at him. *Stop this now. Before something bad happens.*

"Haven…"

"Mmm," she answered, her forehead pressed to his.

"Haven, stop," he managed. "We have to stop."

"In just a…"

"I am serious," he countered. "There is only so much I can withstand."

"It's okay. I'm ready."

"No," he breathed.

"It's fine. I know what I'm saying, what I'm doing."

Colton backed away to the other side of the room. "No," he said again, more firmly.

Haven's lower lip trembled.

As he watched, he thought, *She is going to be the death of me.*

"We have to sleep on it at least," he offered because he couldn't be the one to make her cry. Not now. Not again.

"In separate beds," he added quickly. "Away from each other. Far away. You here. Me in the bunkhouse."

She didn't look quite as hurt as she had a moment ago. She was beginning to consider what he'd said, to believe that he may actually want her.

"I'm going to feel the same way tomorrow," she countered.

"Then, we won't be losing anything," he responded. "If you feel the same way tomorrow, then we will have only increased the anticipation. That's good."

His stress on the word *good* made him sound like a madman. That and the fact that his words were tumbling out of his mouth at a million miles a minute, trying to build a wall between them. This time, it was a wall with a door, but a wall nonetheless. Something had to prevent him from throwing reason and good intentions out the door, so he could indulge in the taste of her sweet lips once more.

"How do I know you won't leave while I am asleep?"

Because wild horses couldn't drag me away, he wanted to stay.

"I'll be here" was what he said instead, thankful that mind reading was a talent only given to superheroes in books and movies.

"Okay," she conceded. "We'll wait."

"Good. Great. Wonderful."

Haven smiled at him. Even she couldn't overlook his nervousness now, ignore its presence in his repetitious speech.

"You want dinner?" she asked.

"Only if we sit on opposite ends of a very long table."

Colton was serious, but Haven couldn't help but laugh.

"I've made stew," she said, sounding like her old self.

"Well, I've never been able to turn down a good stew."

"Good," she answered, dishing up a bowl first for him, then for herself. "Great. Wonderful." She was making fun of him.

He smiled, though, because even these tortured moments in her presence were better than none at all.

Chapter Eighteen

Colton woke up with a start. He was not in the bunkhouse. Not in one of the barns. Not prostrate on the ground, being supported by good ol' Mother Earth.

He was none other than in the main house. Haven's home.

He was afraid he was in trouble with himself. Serious trouble with himself. And with Moira.

Slowly, Colton lifted his head. Looking about, he saw a side table. That was good. His vision was clear. He didn't appear to be hungover or, worse yet, still drunk.

On the side table was a lamp. And what was more important, the side table was down by his feet. Which brought him to another important fact. The headboard was to his back. Except it wasn't a headboard. It was the back of a couch.

This, of course, was excellent news.

What was even better was that there was no Haven in sight. Neither were her full, soft, sweet lips present. Nor her starry eyes. Nor her misplaced trust.

A quick clothing check revealed the good and the bad. Colton decided to refrain from assessing for the ugly. He was too tired for that.

The good: he was not naked. The bad: he was one pair of boxers away from being so.

But at least, those boxers were firmly in place.

Well, not firmly. Thanks to the human habit known as sleeping, they were more than a little askew. Still, they were there, which was more than he could say for many such similar mornings in his past.

Colton sat up and pulled the throw with him. He tucked it under his arms until he could find a shirt.

"You look like a girl," Haven said, startling him, then handing him a hot beverage.

Unsure what else to do, Colton took the mug in his hand and sipped the strong coffee.

Not bright. Hot coffee on unprepared tongue equals ouch.

His heart was hammering in his chest. He hadn't been this nervous since the last time she had made him feel this way. He realized he had to speak. She was waiting for him to say something.

"Do you care to, uh, elaborate about the girl comment?" he asked, giving her the opportunity to steer her remark down Compliment Cul-De-Sac or Insult Lane. It was up to her.

"You know what I am talking about. In the movies. Boy meets girl. Girl falls for boy. Girl and boy spend the night together. Girl covers her chest sheepishly the next morning while boy parades himself around, proud of his nakedness."

Colton cocked his eyebrow. "What kind of movies have you been watching?" He couldn't help but seize the chance to turn the tables. It was what they did to each other when things weren't going well.

Haven tossed a pillow at him. "You know I am right. It happens in films all the time. Probably even in yours."

"Perhaps, Miss Morrow. But I thought you didn't

watch movies."

"I don't. Not often. But that doesn't mean I have never seen one before."

He *tsk-tsk*ed her before speaking. "No wonder you stopped watching them. To have seen such tawdry material and at such a young age. Your friends and family must have been worried about you."

She smirked.

"Pray tell," he continued, pulling an accent of unclear origin out of his hat, "how did they handle your intervention? Was it as impromptu as mine was? Well, as mine were, actually. I seem to have required more than one. Or were there Bibles and thumping and mentions of the words *hell* and *damnation*?"

"You know you can't turn this around on me." She smiled further, taking a sip of her morning brew. "You are embarrassed to be waking up here, wondering what happened. No amount of wordplay is going to get you out of that."

"You're the one who called me a girl."

"You're the one who was acting like one."

"I happen to believe women are exceptional creatures. So, I will take that as a compliment."

Haven laughed into her mug. "I never meant it to be anything less."

"You are feisty in the morning," Colton pointed out, breaking his assumed character.

"It's the stew. Plus, I've had a good night's rest."

"What did you do? Drug us with it?"

It would explain a lot.

"No. My grandmother's stew is the perfect balance of meat, vegetables, broth, and spices. It also happens to aid sleep-deprived cowboys with getting a few extra winks."

"You drugged us."

"I did no such thing."

"You gave us a concoction known to alter the mind and body. That's drugging someone."

She smiled indulgently.

"Might I remind you that I came here to get away from drug pushers and their powerful products?"

"Colton," she continued, refusing to take the bait, "I cooked a comforting meal for myself, and you came up here to yell at me. If anyone, you are to blame for your predicament. I did not force the stew on you."

"I tried to go home."

"You didn't get far," she amended.

"Fine. I messed up. Now, can you just tell me how badly? All I remember is kissing you and arguing. There was quite a bit of arguing. And then, we made some kind of peace. Next, you fed us that devil stew."

"My grandmother's stew."

"Then what? I can't recall a single thing after that."

"You hit on me. I said no. You tried again. I coldcocked you. You were robbed by a pair of traveling ne'er-do-wells and deposited without clothes on my couch."

"Haven…"

"We talked, Colton. That's all. We talked to each other. Nicely, I might add. Then you got tired. I insisted you stay here. You argued a bit before passing out on the couch. I took off your shirt…"

"Haven…"

"Oh, calm down. I only washed it. I washed your pants, too."

Colton's entire face turned red. He'd never been so

interested in what a girl thought about his body or so embarrassed to be obviously wondering.

"Nice pecs," she said, "but you already knew that."

"You're killing me."

"It's payback."

"Payback for what?"

"Making me wait."

"Haven, come on. You have to stop. I am not awake enough for this."

"I am serious. We've slept on it. In separate rooms. I have made my decision. Tonight's the night."

"Is that an order?"

"Sort of."

"You do realize I am not your property."

"No. But you are on my property. And you know what they say…"

"What the landlord wants, she gets?"

"Exactly."

Colton stood up abruptly. "I am going to go take a shower now."

Haven started to direct him to the shower upstairs, but he called out, "In the bunkhouse," as he retreated across the yard in only his boxers, with a throw held firmly against his front.

Mortified, he thought. *I am mortified. And a teensy bit happy. Who knew?*

Chapter Nineteen

For the rest of the day, Colton could feel Haven's eyes on him like a predator sighting its prey. He had no idea how he was going to break the news to her that tonight would not be the night. No matter what he had said the previous evening, he was going to have to renege.

He just wasn't ready.

He was two months sober from substances, but the loss of Haven could send him back to where he had started. And he didn't see how he could be anything close to what she needed.

By the time night was falling, Haven had made dinner for them and ordered him to the main house. He arrived with a bouquet of handpicked wildflowers. He might not be prepared to act in a carnal way, but that didn't mean he couldn't be gentlemanly.

"It's good to see you," Haven said as he walked through the open door.

Every figurative light was green. In Haven's mind, the evening was a go. From the well-laid-out table to the music playing in the background, she had done her best to set the stage. A woman's soft voice crooned, detailing her fall for the wrong man who turned out to be the right man after all.

A track picked especially.

He wondered if the title of Haven's playlist was

Seducing the Resident Bad Boy.

"Everything looks good," Colton said, purposefully looking away from her.

She was obviously the most ravishing part of the evening, but he had no business paying close attention to that.

"Thank you," she said, pulling out a chair for him. It was true what they said about farm girls. They were very good at hospitality. Too good, as far as Colton was concerned.

"So, the cows looked great today," he offered.

"They did," she agreed.

It made him suddenly want to pick a fight. His face must have given him away because Haven asked him if he was all right.

"Sure. Fine. Great."

"Nervous, I see."

"Haven, come on…"

"There is nothing to be nervous about," she said. "You've done this a thousand times."

He looked up at her suddenly.

"I didn't mean…"

He had his in. "Are you saying I am promiscuous?" He inserted as much venom in his voice as he could.

"Colton…"

"No. You're right. I have done this a lot, which is how I know this isn't right for you."

"I am not your child, Colton."

"No. And you're not my girlfriend either." He meant the words to hurt.

Her response did more damage to him than his had done to her. "I don't expect that. I know that's not what you want."

Geez. It's like she's read a book on how to disarm me.

He took a step closer, placed his hands on her arms, and squeezed slightly, sending her eyes up to his. "You are not the problem. You get that, right?" he questioned.

She started to reach for his face again, the most disarming move of all.

He took a step back.

"How did all of those other girls get in your bed?" she asked.

He shared the truth. "They didn't matter."

She didn't so much as flinch. "It's okay if I don't matter."

He didn't tell her that was impossible. Instead, he said, "You should matter to whoever you are with."

"I know I'm not as experienced as you are. But I get that wanting isn't the same as caring."

She was referencing his words, trying to suss out if he felt anything for her.

"Haven, I care about you."

"Is that a problem?"

"Yes."

"Why?"

"Have you ever been at the edge of caring about someone so much that you can't move forward? Knowing that no matter what you do, the relationship between you will never be right?"

"Colton..."

"I can't love you the way you need to be loved, Haven. That doesn't mean I don't feel anything for you. I do. But if I touch you again, hold you for a night, you will be branded into my flesh, absorbed into me in a way that no drug has ever been. And I will crave you for the rest of my life."

"Colton, I am right here."

"Yes. You are. But you haven't been with me and then fought with me. Haven't shared with me all that two people can share, then had me disappoint you endlessly. It's different. That kind of connection, then separation, will make your flesh ache. It will torture your beating heart until you wish the fragile organ would stop beating altogether."

"Colton, I would never—"

"You will," he answered. "All the ones I've ever loved do."

There. He had laid his soul bare. In an effort to keep his body under wraps, he'd exposed the part of himself that he had never wanted her to see.

Haven's eyes bored into his. They sent every ounce of feeling she possessed across the space between them. But she didn't move.

Instead, she waited. Knowing that, now, he couldn't leave. She owned a part of him. And the rest of who he was wanted to be reunited with that part, so the hole in his heart could finally be healed.

Chapter Twenty

Just as Colton was about to cross the space between himself and Haven, there was a knock at the door.

"Sister, I'm home."

Haven turned sharply, her eyes going wide.

"Well, well, well, what have we here?" the intruder drawled, eyeing the accoutrements of a romantic evening gone bust.

Haven's guard went up immediately. Her openness locked away behind some door that only she possessed the key to.

"May I ask who you are?" Colton interjected.

What he really wanted to do was punch the guy in the face. Anybody who could make Haven turn to stone deserved a fist to the jaw.

"Rusty."

"His name is Levi," Haven corrected.

"But I go by Rusty, baby sister. You know that."

Colton balled his hands into fists. They were itching to hurt the louse before him.

"So, can I have some of this grub, or am I interrupting something?"

All of the desire moments ago inhabiting Haven's face had drained away. She looked ready to die. She was embarrassed by Rusty, everything in her being broadcast that fact to the world. How couldn't she be?

He was trying to be an embarrassment and to embarrass her.

"You can have whatever you like," Colton said. "We were just about to go check on the horses."

He pressed his hand to Haven's back and steered her out of the house.

"Not with those candles lit, you weren't." Rusty chuckled.

A hundred yards out, Colton asked potentially the worst question he could ask. "Was he adopted?"

Luckily, Haven laughed.

Maybe he wasn't the only one who had wondered how the girl before him and the brute back at the main house could share a gene pool.

"No, he's not."

"Oh."

Just as they arrived at the barn's main doors, Haven confessed, "He used to be a much different person."

"What happened?" Colton asked.

"Drugs," she sighed. "And movies."

Colton felt the tip of the torpedo enter his chest right before it exploded. "Is that why you don't watch films?"

"Yes," she answered softly.

"I don't mean to be argumentative, but watching too much TV or going to the theater too many times won't change a person."

"No. But falling in love with fame and fortune, then failing to obtain both will."

"He tried to be an actor."

"Yes," she answered, grabbing a sugar cube from the box she kept stashed in the tack room. She walked it over to Cicero.

"I'm sorry," he said.

He could see in her eyes that she was once very close to her brother before he turned.

"There's nothing to be sorry about."

"I am apologizing on behalf of all Hollywood affiliates."

She smiled for a second.

"And former druggies."

"Colton, don't…it's not the same."

"I'm afraid it is," he disagreed. "I have been just as callous as he was back there. To many people. Even been worse."

"But you wouldn't be to me."

"Didn't you once believe that your brother wouldn't hurt you?"

It was Haven's turn to be wounded.

"I'm sorry," he said. "I'm not trying to make this worse. I just want you to know that a person who is under the influence is very different from one who is sober."

"You wouldn't hurt me, Colton."

"I wouldn't want to," he said. "At least, that we can agree on."

Chapter Twenty-One

Colton and Haven ended up hanging around the barn for a long time, each trying to keep amiable conversation going. Colton did his best to be there for Haven while trying to avoid the intimacy she had created earlier with her well-laid-out romantic dinner.

"Why exactly does Levi go by Rusty?" he asked.

"It's a nickname he got on one of his first movie sets. It just stuck."

"I thought he was a failed actor."

"He was working as an extra."

"Is that what he still does now?"

"No. He auditions for stuff. But Levi doesn't apply himself. He's never studied acting. He just wants access to the money and the babes, as he calls them."

"So what does he do, then?"

"Mostly?"

Colton nodded his head.

"He shows up here when he needs money, pulling the family card."

"Do you know when to expect him?"

"No. Never."

Haven stared at her fingers, which were breaking down a stalk of hay into thin strips of next to nothingness.

"I get what you must be feeling."

"What?" she asked.

"Embarrassment."

She looked up at him, checking to make sure that he was referencing her brother and not the night that she had planned.

"I mean about your brother," he clarified.

"Yeah." She shrugged. "Sometimes."

"Do you miss him when he is gone?"

"I miss a person that isn't there anymore, one that no longer exists."

Colton waited a minute before asking the next question. "What kind of drugs was he on, if you don't mind?"

"What kind wasn't he on? He's tried everything. Said it helps him with his craft."

"Has he ever been in rehab?"

"Multiple times."

"No wonder you flipped out when you thought I was using."

Haven smiled a sad smile.

"I know this might be a weird question," he said, reaching up to scratch Cicero behind the ears, "but how can you deal with me being here, considering…"

"It's different."

"I'm not sure it's as different as you think…"

"For one, you didn't leave me to take care of our sick mother on my own…"

"I did bug out and leave the farm the other day…"

"For another, you have talent. I know I'm not a Colton Grey aficionado, but Moira wouldn't have done everything she's done if she didn't believe in you."

"Who's to say—"

"Finally, I can see inside of you. I can't explain it. But I can."

"What does that mean?"

"It means what I told you before. I know you would never hurt me. Not on purpose."

"Does Rusty, I mean Levi, hurt you on purpose?"

"When we were kids, he didn't. He would never. Now that we are adults, he cuts me down every chance he gets."

"That's horrible."

"He's doing it out of pain. On some level, he's disappointing himself."

"That doesn't give him the right..."

"No, it doesn't. "

Colton watched her stare at her beloved companion, a creature with four legs who would never do her wrong. She was so beautiful. So caring. So...

"Colton, what's wrong?"

He could feel his cheeks turning red as visions of kissing her overtook his mind. "Nothing," he responded curtly.

"You went pale and now you're red."

"I...I'm fine."

She reached up to touch his forehead, to check for a fever. It was a loving gesture. A caring gesture. An innocent one, too.

But suddenly, he had to be away from her. Because all he wanted to do was take her in his arms. Not in the way she had planned before. Not as an act of desire. More as an act of complete and total supplication. He wanted to kneel at the altar of everything he felt and worship in the way his body now knew it was meant to worship.

Which wasn't him.

Colton was used to playing the love-besotted

scoundrel, not being him.

Haven had him in way over his head. No matter his thoughts, no matter his feelings, he had to break free. This would only end in heartbreak, for her and likely him too.

The emergence of Levi was proof of that. Haven was much more fragile than she seemed to be. Why wouldn't she be?

Everyone around her has disappointed her. And now, I will too. But at least, if I leave immediately, it will be in a way far less damaging than it could have been.

Colton half expected to hear Haven rushing after him. But no footsteps followed his. All he could make out were his own strides pounding the earth below his feet.

When he neared the bunkhouse, he found that his drive to secure Haven's emotional survival sent him past his sleeping quarters. In fact, it sent him right up to the main house.

Colton yanked open the screen door and allowed it to slam shut after him. "Levi."

"The name's Rusty, man," Haven's brother slurred.

Colton turned the corner into the kitchen to see Levi helping himself to Haven's feast. He was taking no care to preserve any of the food for others either. Levi was going in for seconds with used utensils. Eventually, he gave up on summoning coordination in his inebriated state and started picking up a selection of roasted potatoes with his fingers.

"Levi," Colton said, refusing to play into the Rusty character Haven's brother had taken on as a way to get through life, "you better take care of your sister."

"Why, so you can split?"

Anger rose in his chest because a part of the dolt's comment was true. Colton did want to leave. Desperately. "You know what I mean."

"I only know what I see, bro. And what I see is a passerby, moving in on my sister, then leaving her out to dry."

"I have done nothing to your sister."

"If you haven't yet, it is only a matter of time. Look at this spread," he said, gesturing. "She was offering herself up to you, am I right?"

Colton was sick to his stomach. How any man could talk about his sister in that way was beyond him.

"I would never hurt your sister."

"I'm pretty sure you already have."

Colton turned around to see Haven standing in the doorway. She looked furious. And so very sad.

"Haven, I—"

"Colton, please leave. I will take care of this."

"I was just trying to help."

"I understand what you were trying to do. Now, go."

Colton did as he was told, walking out the door. If he had a tail, it would have been tucked sheepishly between his legs.

He'd meant to protect Haven. But, somehow, he seemed to have made things worse.

Chapter Twenty-Two

"Moira," Colton whispered into the telephone. "Call me as soon as you get this. Something's up. I'm worried about Haven."

Two hours later, Moira's call came in. "Colton. Colton, are you there?"

"Yes," he answered, fighting what sounded like helicopter blades for Moira's attention. "Where are you?"

"I'm at a helipad sending a client out of the country for a bit."

"May I ask why?"

"No, you may not. I don't know why you celebrities all seem to crash at the same time, but you do."

A worried man's voice came over the line.

"Not you, George," Moira called out, muffling the phone. "Your helicopter is not going to crash. You'll be just fine."

"Fear of flying?" Colton asked when she returned to the line.

"Fear of following orders is more like it."

"A man after my own heart," Colton said, his smooth ways coming back to him.

"So, what's up, Colton? You sounded distressed the last time you called."

"I'm glad that modern voicemail can capture the

tenor of a caller's dynamic array of emotions."

"Cut the crap, Mr. Grey. What's going on?"

"Colton Grey," the man boarding the helicopter called out. "Is that Colton Grey you have on the line?"

"Pay attention to your life, George. Before it goes up in smoke," Moira called.

"I am not sure I like seeing this bossy side of you used on other clients," Colton teased. "I thought you were only a tyrant with me. You're making me jealous."

"Colton, please. I am juggling a lot right now. What's going on with Haven?"

"I have two syllables for you. Le-vi."

"Levi's back in town?"

"Yes."

"Then, you have to help her."

"Moira, I was planning on leaving."

"You can't leave. You mustn't. Trust me."

"What is that supposed to mean?"

"It means you have to find a way to get him to hit the road again before I can come get you."

"I don't think that's the best idea—" Colton began.

"I am serious. Levi is bad news."

"I believe you."

"Then what's the problem? I know you don't want Haven to get hurt."

Colton refused to tell her that Haven had set her sights on him. He just couldn't.

"This problem is a little more complicated than you think," he offered instead. "It comes with a side of extra villain."

"I'm sorry. I'm not following."

"Levi has an alter ego named Rusty. He is worse

than the original, I think, though I don't know much about either."

"All you need to know is that Haven needs you right now."

"She already kicked me out of the house."

"Again?"

"No. It was off the farm before. Now, it's just out of the main house. Do keep up."

"Why is no one normal?" Moira sighed.

"I don't think that's an okay way to speak about Haven."

"I am not talking about Haven. I am talking about you. Can't you see that Haven is embarrassed? That she's trying to keep the depth of her family's problems from you?"

"Yes."

"Then why are you letting that stop you?"

"Boundaries," Colton replied. "Those precious structures you lectured me about the entire way here."

"You weren't coherent. I had to repeat myself."

"Well, the repetition worked. Boundaries are all I can think about every time I see Haven or talk to her or have a conversation about her—"

"Look. I wasn't planning on doing this," Moira began, "but apparently I am going to have to."

"Do what?"

"Pull out the schoolyard orders. You will not be leaving that farm until you fix this situation with Rusty. I forbid it."

"So, we are calling him Rusty now?" Colton chose to ignore the dictator-like decree.

"Levi. Rusty. Peter, Peter the Pumpkin Eater. I don't care."

"Relying on nursery rhymes, are we? This regression runs deep. When shall the noogies and wet willies commence?"

"Just fix this, Colton. Please. I know it's not your job. Just think of it as repayment for the million second chances you have been given."

With that, the fight left Colton. "All right," he said. "I'll help."

"Good," she replied. "Call me when it's done."

"Shall I reach you on a Bond-style phone in an MI6-worthy helicopter?"

"For all I know, I will be in Bunker One."

"Bunker One?"

"It's my nickname for the President's bunker."

"Like Air Force One?"

"Yes."

"Moira."

"Mm-hmm."

"Don't quit your day job. Script writing is not for you."

Moira laughed, then hung up the phone.

Colton put his head in his hands and ran his fingers through his hair. Now, he had a mission. One he had to complete without the aid of drugs, alcohol, or even sanity.

As it turned out, his respite from the entertainment world could be the thing that drove him fully over the edge rather than pulled him back from it.

Chapter Twenty-Three

Colton heard a knock at the bunkhouse door. "Who is it?" he called.

Instead of answering, Haven walked inside. "Hey," she said sheepishly.

"Hi," he answered, rubbing sleep out of his eyes.

He'd spent half the night trying to come up with a plan for getting Levi to leave the farm peacefully. So far, all he had to show for his efforts was an imagined Charlie-Chaplin-style montage where he kicked Levi in the rear and Levi went flying.

His plan was clearly none too light on the fantastic.

"Levi still here?"

"Yes," she answered.

"You okay?"

"Yeah. I'm fine."

"You don't sound it."

Haven ignored him. "Are you planning on getting out of bed any time soon?"

It took everything in him not to point out that, last night, prior to her brother's arrival, all she had been trying to do was to get him in bed.

"Colton?"

"Yes," he drew out.

"Seriously. Are you going to get up or what?"

"Or what."

"You're really not going to help out today at all?"

"I am."

"When?"

"In another couple of hours."

"What has you so tired today?"

You. Thinking of you. Trying not to think of you. Wanting to figure out how to save you. Wanting to figure out how to walk away from saving you. You.

"Hollywood business," he lied.

"News about the movie?"

"Moira called. Said I needed to stay here for a bit longer. I guess they aren't quite comfortable with my sobriety yet."

"You are welcome here, Colton. For however long it takes. Despite what I told Moira before."

"I know."

"There's just one catch," she added.

"Why do I think I am not going to like this catch?"

"All guests must earn their keep."

She pushed with her boot at the metal frame that housed the mattress on which he lay.

"I suppose you are telling me that I need to get out of bed right now."

"No. I am telling you that you needed to be out of bed two hours ago."

Colton failed to do so much as stretch his pinky. "What time is it anyway?"

"Time for you to get moving."

He chuckled. "I am starting to see the family resemblance."

Haven took a step back.

"Between you and Moira," he added, not wanting her to misconstrue his meaning.

Haven softened. "Oh. Well, yes, she can be quite

the taskmaster."

"Did you teach her or did she teach you?"

"A little bit of both, I think."

Colton smiled. "I promise I'll get up if you do one thing for me."

"What's that?"

"Give me a second to throw on some clothes."

"Okay."

"Alone."

"Oh, right. Uh, sorry."

"I'll meet you out front in five."

Haven looked a bit embarrassed. After she turned around, she whispered over her shoulder. "Colton?"

"Yes."

"Thanks for last night."

"No problem."

She turned back to face him, staring him straight in the eye. "No, seriously. Thank you."

"It was my pleasure."

"I shouldn't have gotten mad at you."

"You were fine."

"I know that you were just trying to protect me."

"I was."

"People don't often do that for me. I'm not used to it. It's normally the other way around."

Colton smiled a sad smile at her. "Any time you need protecting, I'll be there."

She nodded, then walked out of the bunkhouse door.

Colton rolled over and groaned into his pillow. He should have pulled the ripcord on this ranch adventure the moment he saw her. The longer he stayed, the further he fell. There were no two ways about it.

Chapter Twenty-Four

Colton did not like Levi. At all.

Or Rusty. Whoever was in charge now.

The guy seemed content to sit on his porch, chewing on a piece of hay, while his sister slaved away on the farm. Deplorable.

Haven did a good job of ignoring his presence. But when she caught sight of him nodding off in her mother's rocking chair, even she had to resist the urge to hurl her pitchfork at him.

"I wish I understood him," she muttered.

"I don't think there's much to understand."

"He used to be a decent person."

Colton refrained from telling her that Levi was probably always a bad seed. In the short time he'd known him, he couldn't find a single redeemable quality.

After a bit, a trembling voice asked, "Do you think I did something wrong?"

There were unmistakable tears in her eyes.

Colton set down the buckets of water he had been hauling and went to her. He rested his hands on her upper arms and willed her to look into his eyes. "No, Haven. You didn't."

Then, against his better judgment, he pulled her into a hug, kissing the top of her head for good measure. He'd thrown out the rulebook. He was acting on instinct now. "His problems have absolutely nothing to do with you," he added.

"I don't understand…"

"There's nothing to understand. He serves himself. He might not have been this way in the past. He may not be this way in the future. But for now, all he can see is himself. No one else matters. No one even registers as a person."

"I'm not sure how much more of this I can take."

"Just say the word, and I will make him leave," Colton whispered.

"I can't," Haven said with a sob. "I just can't."

Colton pulled her in a little tighter, letting her cry herself out. Then he installed her on a bench in the alleyway of the barn and went to the house to grab a glass of iced tea that she could drink.

On Colton's way in, Levi muttered, "I see you use every opportunity to get closer to my sister."

"Listen, *man*," Colton said, making the word *man* sound more like *half-brained, nitwitted, juvenile oaf* than any kind of assertion of his masculinity or maturity, "you need to lay off. Of me and your sister. We are not the problem here."

"Really? That's not what I heard."

"I'll let you finish your statement. I can tell you are one who craves a dramatic pause."

"As far as I've heard, you're here on the farm to sober up."

"At least, I've made an attempt to get better."

"It's not hard to pretend to be sober when all you've done is trade one addiction for another," Levi stated, letting his eyes drift to the barn where Haven was waiting.

"You are a piece of work," Colton said.

What he wanted to do was punch the guy in the face. He was ridiculous. Insinuating he could ever use Haven in any way. Mess up? Maybe. But use her? Never.

"I'm here to protect what's mine."

"Haven doesn't belong to you."

"She doesn't belong to you either."

"No. You're right. She doesn't belong to me. She doesn't belong to anyone but herself. Something you wouldn't understand."

Levi chuckled. "Are you saying I am not my own man?"

"I am saying you are in the grips of something I can only think of as evil."

"You would know, brother."

"Don't call me your brother."

"It's an expression."

"Any reference to the fact that I so much as have to breathe the same air as you is out of bounds at this point."

"Touchy. Touchy."

Colton wanted to tell him to leave. Hell, he wanted to escort him off the ends of the Earth. But Haven couldn't deal with that now.

At this point, no matter her momentary wavering, she still believed. In Levi. In herself. In the ability of good to conquer the worst in the world.

What she didn't understand was that bad wouldn't change if it didn't want to. A wolf in sheep's clothing was still a wolf. And it was clear, Levi had no desire to shed his bristly hide and start anew.

No. He was here to take advantage of Haven one

last time. And by the gleam in his eyes, this heist would be his biggest one yet.

Chapter Twenty-Five

Colton spoke into the receiver as softly as he could.

Haven was nearby. She had wandered down to the bunkhouse at about midnight and asked if she could sleep in the bed next to his. He'd said yes, secretly glad that she had wanted to put at least a little distance between herself and her miscreant brother.

The problem was her presence made checking in with Moira more difficult.

Previously, he'd been texting her throughout the day. But eventually, Haven had become suspicious. So he'd arranged to have a chat with Moira via cell at about the time that Haven had shown up to request to sleep in the bunkhouse with him.

Immediately, he'd texted, *Abort mission*, to which Moira had replied, *Training for another role?*

He'd hardy-har-harred in his head but hadn't typed it for two reasons. One, Haven would have suspected something was up. Two, who typed *hardy-har-har* anyway?

On the porch, Colton had to will himself not to pace or tap his foot or throw his cell phone into a nearby water trough when Moira failed to answer for the fourth time.

He was about to call it a night and head to bed when his cell phone finally vibrated.

"Moira? Is that you? I've left you four messages."

"Have you forgotten how to use caller ID?" she asked, ignoring the chiding portion of his remark.

"No. Have you forgotten how caller ID works? You aren't calling from your usual number. Well, your most recent burner anyway."

"Oh. Right. I stole Geoffrey's phone."

"Geoffrey? As in in Gee-off-ree Geoffrey?"

"I know how it's pronounced now, thank you."

"Thanks to me."

"You're right. Thanks to you." Moira quickly seized her opportunity. "Speaking of thanks to you, have you kicked Levi to the curb yet?"

"No."

"What? Why not?"

"Haven doesn't want him to leave."

"You do understand that Haven hasn't accepted what an arsehole that guy is, don't you?"

"Arsehole? Geoffrey rubbing off on you? He's working on a British piece, isn't he?"

"Yes and no."

Just then, Colton heard "Tallyho!" shouted in the background.

He couldn't help it. Just like Moira, he clutched at the chance that the universe had given him. "Do explain, Moira. This does sound like a tasty bit of news."

"Not that it is any of your business," Moira stated, knowing she would get nowhere if she didn't give in to Colton's demands, "but Geoffrey had a wee bit of an accident."

"And?"

"And now, he thinks he's British."

"I know this isn't right to say, not after he's had the

kind of incident he's had, but for some reason, I can picture him running through the halls of a mental ward in a sleeping gown from the eighteenth century."

"You're right except for the eighteenth-century sleeping gown part."

"He's in a mental ward?"

"A state-of-the-art neuropsychological facility actually."

"I am surprised you are telling me all of this."

"It's going to print tomorrow."

"You let something as big as a mental breakdown hit the papers?"

"No. Geoffrey called a press conference to discuss reuniting with the Motherland."

"He wants us to rejoin Great Britain?"

"Something like that."

"Where do you get your clients, Moira?"

"Same place I found you. Crazytown, USA, otherwise known as Los Angeles."

"I thought you were going to say Tinseltown."

"Too many towns in one sentence."

Colton laughed. Then, he heard Haven stir.

"Listen, Moira, I am enjoying catching up. But I really do need help with Haven."

"It doesn't sound like there is much I can do if you refuse to get rid of Levi."

"I was thinking, maybe, you could get him a small part. He'd leave the farm then. I am sure of it."

"I've got enough wackos on my roster right now."

"Come on, Moira. You and I both know he can't hack it for long. You'd only need to pull your strings for a little while, leak some good information about him to the press, set him up with my agent. She owes me one."

"Drug problems and identity crises are one thing, Colton. Sociopathy is quite another."

"It's not like he clubs baby seals."

"How would you know? Have you interviewed all of the baby seals along the California coast?"

"Please, Moira."

"Last time I heard you pleading like that, I was dragging you away from a roomful of naked models and copious amounts of powdery white substances."

"Don't remind me." The more time Colton spent around Levi, the more he was ashamed of himself.

"You do know you're nothing like him, right?" Moira asked.

"I'm not so sure," he answered, toeing the edge of a board beneath his foot.

"You're not, Colton. You lost your way."

"And Levi?"

"He was never good to begin with."

"Then how can she still care about him?"

"Haven is loyal above all else. And he's family."

Colton was beginning to think this whole enterprise was useless. Then Moira did the unthinkable and agreed to represent Levi.

"Thanks, Moira. You won't regret this."

"I think we both will, Colton. You do know I am going to use your name to sell him. Say he is the next you."

Colton looked at Haven, noticed how peacefully she breathed in her sleep. "Do whatever you have to do. I don't care if I never work another day in this town as long as she is safe."

Moira hesitated before saying, "I never thought I'd

see the day you fell in love."

"Neither did I," he said, realizing just after she'd hung up that his publicist had just forced him to admit that he was in love with her cousin.

Chapter Twenty-Six

"I was thinking we could take a ride today," Colton said as soon as he noticed Haven stirring.

He'd been propped up on his elbow, watching her sleep for twenty minutes.

"Really? I was thinking we could stay in bed all day," she answered, pulling the covers closer around her body.

"You? Stay in bed? Won't you flog yourself for that or something?"

"The punishment can only follow the crime. I was thinking about enjoying the crime first."

"If that's what you want…" Colton agreed hesitantly.

He studied Haven for signs of depression.

Her skin was glowing. Like it always was. She didn't seem to have added or lost any weight. Her hair was perfectly mussed. That was a sure sign her strands were fighting the good fight.

"Relax, Colton. I'm fine."

"I wasn't—"

"You were looking for signs of an impending breakdown."

"No," he disagreed. "I was simply noting how nice your hair looks in the morning."

"It looks like a rat's nest."

"Wrong," he said, biting his lip so he didn't break

out laughing. "It looks like a very elegant bird's nest."

Oh, to be the one to make her hair look like that, Colton thought to himself.

"You find birds' nests embarrassing or something?" Haven said as she stretched atop the bed.

Birds' nests? No, he thought. *Wanting you more than is humanly bearable while you stretch innocently across from me? Ding ding ding ding ding.*

"Colton?"

"Uh. What?"

"You spaced out."

"No. No, I didn't."

"Yes, you did. And you are turning bright red."

It wasn't just his face that was reacting to the girl before him.

"Colton. Earth to Colton."

"Yes. What?" he asked, perturbed.

She was interrupting his thoughts of baseball and grandmothers and anything else remotely unsexual that he could come up with.

"Colton? I'm serious. Are you going to get up?"

"I thought you wanted to stay in bed."

"I did want to stay in bed. But you made me feel guilty."

"I hardly think you can blame your change of mind on me."

"That's my story and I'm sticking to it."

"Fine," he answered. "But I'm going to need a minute."

"Tired?"

"Something like that," he said.

"Okay. I'll shower first."

"I'll meet you up at the big house."

"I'm going to shower here."

"You don't have any clothes..." he began. That's when he noticed a bag at the end of her bed. She must have run up to the main house to collect some of her things while he was sleeping.

For a second, Colton thought to ask if Levi had hurt her. Maybe he had hit her, and that's why she had come down to the bunkhouse. But he didn't see any additional bruises. The ones her mother had left were fading. And he was pretty sure Haven's loyalty would have cracked at the first sign of intentional domestic violence.

Since Haven couldn't sense the tenor of his thoughts, she teased him as she headed out the door. She promised to use up all of the hot water so he wouldn't have any left for his shower.

Colton didn't mind, however. He would need a heck of a lot of cold water to get him through the day ahead.

Chapter Twenty-Seven

Atop a galloping horse, it should have been easy for Colton to keep his mind in check. Except it wasn't.

All he could think of were Haven's lips when she smiled, her eyes when she laughed, the feel of her skin on his. Several times, she'd grabbed his hand and squeezed it for no reason.

It had taken every ounce of his energy not to focus on getting her alone and finishing what she kept unintentionally starting.

Somehow, something inside of him had been unleashed. Between Moira's insistence on pointing out the obvious and his own desire to protect his publicist's cousin, Colton could only think of Haven. Except his thoughts weren't just of the protective variety. Her past advances had triggered a constant awareness of her body and its effect on him. Colton felt like the starving vampire he had once played who had finally spotted a young maiden alone on an island just as he'd thought he was about to die from thirst.

Die as best a vampire can anyway.

The only difference was he didn't want to devour Haven. Not in the literal sense. Not in the way the vampire devoured the nameless girl. Colton shook his head to rid it of the image.

"You okay?" Haven called back, twisting a bit in her saddle.

"Yes," he answered stoically.

"You've been in your head all morning."

He looked out at the horizon.

"Are you hatching an evil plan? Are you going to steal my farm away from me? Was all of your help just a ruse?"

"No," Colton replied, barely able to say the next part. "I was wondering, Haven, if you would ever consider—I mean, have you ever thought about living…uh…somewhere other than here. The farm, I mean."

Haven halted her horse. Colton continued to walk Ol' Faithful until she was side by side with Cicero.

"Do you not like the farm anymore?"

"No. Yes. Of course I do. That's not what I meant."

"I know you have to leave. You can't stay here forever. Not with the movie and your, um, responsibilities. But I thought you were beginning to like being here…with me."

She looked to be out of breath. Something was stealing the air from her lungs.

She feels it, too, he thought. *This feeling that's killing me.* "Haven, I was just…with your mom sick…I thought maybe you'd like to…come…stay with me. I thought you'd like to stay with me when I go to shoot my movie."

"I have to work on the farm. I can't afford to hire—"

"I can get someone to look after it."

"I can't take any more of your money, Colton. I've already accepted too much."

He reached over to take her hand. When she

132

wouldn't look up at him, he tipped her chin so her eyes could meet his.

"You didn't take anything I didn't want to give."

"I took more than I should have. My problems are not your problems."

"That's what I'm trying to tell you."

"I don't understand."

"I want your problems to be my problems, Haven. I think…no, I mean I know…I'm falling in love with you."

She stopped breathing. Her eyes immediately moistened. Her cheeks pinkened to his favorite shade in the world.

"I don't want to leave," he added. "But I can't stay. Not forever. I'm under contract."

His words were rushing out, trying to do whatever it was they needed to do to get her chest to expand with air again.

"I know," she responded, taking a deep breath.

"If I could move the farm out to LA, I would," he added.

She laughed at this. Colton's train of thought was often impractical. Much different from hers.

"Colton, we could always…I mean…you get weekends off, right?"

"Not on a movie set. Most weeks, we work six or seven days."

"You could visit…when you were done."

"I want more than that, Haven. I am sitting here, thinking about you day and night. I wasn't supposed to. Moira told me not to. But—"

"She told you not to what?" Haven asked, hurt evident in her voice.

"She told me, if I hurt you in any way, she would feed me to the lions at the San Diego Zoo."

"That does sound like Moira." Haven looked down. Her cheeks coloring further. No longer were they tinted by the rush of love. Now, they were tinged by the red of true embarrassment.

Colton thought he understood. "It's okay," he stated quickly, "if you don't feel the same. I know you have only been wanting some relief, a break from everything with the farm and your mom."

"It isn't that." She stopped him. "I do care about you."

She hadn't said *love*. That's all Colton heard, all he could comprehend. She hadn't said she loved him. She had said she cared about him.

Despite what he'd said, not hearing *love* didn't feel okay. It wasn't okay. Before she could increase the depth of his pain, he changed the subject. "Maybe we should head back to the barn. I think it's going to rain."

"Colton, please."

"I'm serious. I can feel water droplets."

It was true. There were droplets of water. But that wasn't what was driving him back to the barn.

Haven didn't argue, however. She drove her horse Cicero into a gallop, careful to steer him along the path they had come. It appeared she was giving him the opportunity to secure a little more grip in the rain.

Colton drove Ol' Faithful past Cicero. He sought to keep himself ahead of Haven, his heart threatening to hammer its way out of his chest. He'd done it again. Participated in breaking his own heart. This was why guys didn't say they loved girls. As soon as they did, girls always set about crushing them to a pulp.

His breakup from Anna had been bad. But this? This was worse. He'd never thought he could feel like this. Not ever. No matter what the scripts had said. No matter what the directors had asked him to project, pulling inspiration from a nonexistent memory.

Colton had never known love could feel like this. Such sweet agony. The kind of feeling you wanted to banish from your system at the same time you asked it to sink into your marrow so it could infect every cell that would ever circulate through your veins from now until the end of time.

The kind of sensation enveloping him now was the kind capable of killing a person. Or of driving him to do things that he had sworn to her he would never do. Not again.

Chapter Twenty-Eight

Colton rushed into the barn with Ol' Faithful in tow. Haven, for once, was behind him.

Both were drenched. They yanked their saddles from their mounts' backs and set them, horn to ground, so that they stuck straight up in the air. This was the best way to get them to dry out quickly. The saddle blankets they threw over the stall doors.

Once they'd toweled off their horses, they had no choice but to face each other.

"Colton, I—" Haven began, weaving the cloth she had used to dry Cicero between the bars of one of the largest stalls in the barn as she spoke. He wasn't fooled. She needed something to do with her hands. Letting a person down was never easy.

"Please. Stop. I'm fine," Colton argued.

"No. Listen," she countered, reaching her hand out to touch his arm.

The sensation burned. White-hot electricity shot up his arm. Fire blazed from his gaze.

When her eyes locked on his, it was all over. He grabbed her, pulled her into his arms, and kissed her like he had never kissed a woman before. He didn't care if she didn't love him. He only needed her to want him. Only wanted her to crave him enough to satiate at least a portion of his yearning.

The problem was, with each kiss, with each

slanting of his mouth over hers, he wanted more, not less. He needed more, not less.

For what felt like hours, Colton's mouth was upon Haven's. Her breath mingled with his. They existed as one being. His hands ran themselves over her frame, touching skin whenever and wherever they could.

When he placed his palm underneath her shirt, flat against her back, she leaned further into him, sending her fingers through his hair. Forcefully, she clutched the back of his neck, pulling him closer to her.

Colton was afraid he was going to do what was once forbidden to him right here on the barn floor. Such was the power his desire had over him now. Such was his attraction to this girl.

So he pulled back, resting his forehead on hers for just a second before putting a few inches between their bodies. He continued to hold her hands, however. He couldn't quite let go.

"What's wrong?" she asked, speaking to their hands, unable to meet his eyes.

"I…you…"

"I want this."

He stared at her.

"Colton. Please. I want this."

With her desire-saturated gaze burning a hole right through him, he breathed, "We're in a barn."

It was all he could think of. With her looking the way she did, looking at him the way she was. Pupils dilated, lips swollen and pink, pleading in her eyes.

She was drunk on their kissing. As was he.

He was losing the battle. It might still be cycling in his veins, sending him toward yes, then yanking him back to no. But he was losing his grip on what was right. He was spiraling further and further into what his body told him was necessary. The temptation was too much to bear.

"I shouldn't...I can't..." he whispered. These words were his last-ditch effort. "I...Haven..." He was begging her to release him from this decision, to help him be a good guy here.

But she couldn't see that, couldn't hear the torture in his voice. All she could process was *shouldn't* and *can't* and the sound of her name as he was asking her to stop.

Pain flitted across her features. She looked as though she had been slapped. He could see the tension from her internal struggle straightening her spine, preparing her for a life-crushing wound, for the inerasable damage of another rejection. She was feeling the same way he had felt only a short while ago when he had said he loved her and she had replied that she cared for him.

Colton couldn't watch the pain swallow her whole. He took a step forward to comfort her. In response, she took a step back. She was preparing to run.

Colton forced the words that would devour his soul if they had no effect through his lips. He had to. He couldn't risk her leaving never to return again. Not knowing what he now knew.

"That's not...uh, Haven...this is so hard. I want to be the good guy here. I want you. I do. Please see that I do. With every fiber of my unworthy being. I want this. I want you more than anything I have ever wanted in my entire life. I just..."

"You want me?"

"Yes," he breathed.

"You promise that you want me?"

"Yes. God, yes."

"Then be with me," she begged.

"What if I…I mean I could mess—"

"I'm choosing you, Colton. Please. Let me choose you."

His last bit of resolve snapped. He nodded his head. "Okay."

With a sigh of relief, she walked into his embrace. He caught a glimpse of her body through her sodden shirt, before she pressed herself into him. The sight of her, even just the bit that he was able to see through the transparent portions of her blouse, was enough to drive him to a state of madness. But they were in a barn. And gentlemen didn't allow women to give themselves to them in the middle of a barn.

Plus, their location wasn't the only problem. Her brother was still on the farm, sure to turn up at the wrong moment. Such seemed to be his specialty.

Just as Colton was about to kiss Haven again, almost as if on cue, footsteps could be heard at the end of the walkway.

"I'm sorry to interrupt," Levi drawled. "But there's a call for you."

Haven reached for the phone.

"For him," Levi corrected, handing the phone to Colton.

Perturbed, he put the receiver to his ear.

"Colton Grey here."

"Colton. It's me, Moira. Are you alone?"

"Yes. Haven's right here beside me," he answered in as sweet a tone as he could muster. His didn't match Moira's voice, which sounded urgent.

"Can you step away for a second?"

"Sure. Haven and I just finished our ride. She won't mind if I hash out some contract stuff with you, will you, Haven?"

Haven shook her head though her whole body looked defeated.

Colton walked quickly out of the barn.

Once he was sure he was out of earshot, he barked at Moira. "What's going on?"

"Levi's taken a loan out on the farm."

"What do you mean he's taken a loan out on the farm?"

"He went to visit his mom. Haven's mom. Their mom." Moira was having difficulty speaking. She was rattled. "He had her sign over power of attorney, Colton. Then he took a loan out on the farm."

"Surely, her doctors wouldn't have let her—"

"She's in bad shape. Has been for years. Levi probably pulled his whole loving son act. Everyone outside of the family buys it, for a while at least."

"Can't Haven have it reversed? Turn the money back in. Cancel the loan."

"It's not that simple. He's already blown a portion of it renting a house out here in Malibu."

"What?" Colton asked.

"I told him I could get him some work. Like we talked about."

"Nothing will pay him enough to rent a place out in Malibu. Not a house anyway."

"That's why he got the loan."

"Moira, this will break Haven's heart. She's been happy to be bill free for a while. It's lifted a weight off her shoulders."

"I know," Moira said.

"How did he do this so quickly?"

"He got the power of attorney signed as soon as his mom went into the hospital."

"And the loan?"

"The Morrows have a lot of land, Colton. It makes for good collateral."

"Has he done this before?"

"Nothing this bad…"

"There's something else, isn't there?"

"Yes," she answered hesitantly.

"What? What is it?"

"He's put the place up for sale."

"He can't," Colton shouted. "The farm doesn't belong to him."

"As their mother's guardian, he can do whatever he likes."

"This seems cruel even for him."

"He's never cared about the farm the way Haven does. He'll be glad to get rid of it."

"How are you going to tell her?" Colton asked, all color draining from his face.

"I'm not," she answered.

"What do you mean, you're not?"

"You are, Colton. You're there. You can comfort her."

He couldn't tell her that he was about to do something far less noble than comfort her cousin only moments ago.

"Moira?"

"Yes, Colton."

"You think you can get me off a murder rap?"

"Let's not test the limits of my abilities."

"You don't think public opinion would be with me on this?"

"I am sure it would. But public opinion is not legal opinion."

"Right," he muttered. "You're right." Then he added, "I'm not sure Haven would forgive me for killing her brother anyway."

Moira chuckled. "Probably not."

"Moira?"

"Yes?"

"Thanks for letting me know."

"You're welcome," she replied. "Let me know once you've told her, okay?"

"I will."

"Good-bye."

"Bye," he muttered, then mashed the end call button to disconnect the phone.

Chapter Twenty-Nine

Colton walked into the barn to see Levi taking on yet another personality. This one of animal lover and ranch hand. He threw a flake of hay to Cicero and to a sorrel mare nearby.

"Have you told her?" Colton called as he strode up to Levi.

"Have I told her what?" Levi asked innocently.

"That you went and saw your mother."

"You saw Mom?" Haven asked. "How was she?"

"She's fine. Getting better every day. The doctors say she won't have to stay in as long as usual this time."

"That's good," Haven said, trying to diffuse the obvious tension between Colton and Levi. "It's okay if he sees Mom on his own."

"That's not the most interesting part of his visit."

Levi's eyes burned with the hatred of those called out for their actions.

"Tell her what you had your mother sign while you were there."

Haven blinked twice, unsure of what Colton knew and what had transpired between her brother and her mother.

"Tell me, Levi. I am sure it's okay." She was slipping into her caring sister routine, all irritation at him fading away with each second.

"It's not okay," Colton spit, willing the situation to turn on its head. "Tell her."

"I had Mom sign over power of attorney."

"Why?" Haven asked, her lips frozen on the last syllable.

"So he could take out a loan on the ranch."

"He couldn't possibly…" Haven stated, turning to Colton.

The truth was written all over his face.

"That was Moira who called?" she asked, a crack in her voice.

"Yes," Colton answered.

"Why didn't she call…how did she find out…why would you do this?" She finally turned to Levi. "I just…Colton just…things were finally looking up. Why would you do this to me and to Mom, to our family?"

"I needed a place to stay," Levi replied.

"You have a place to stay, here on the farm."

"In Malibu."

"Malibu? What will you be doing in Malibu?"

"Moira finally got me a part."

"Moira?" Haven turned to Colton. "Why is Moira helping Levi?"

"Because I asked her to," Colton answered.

"Why would you ask her to get him a part?"

Colton hesitated before admitting, "So he would leave the farm."

"I told you I was okay with him being here."

"You don't see him for who he is."

"A screw-up like you, right, Hollywood? Someone destined to break her heart."

"I would never hurt her." Colton rounded on Levi. "I am nothing like you."

"You are everything like me. Except you're not related to her. That makes you afraid. You are worried that Haven will be more loyal to me than she is to you."

"This isn't some sick game, Levi. I care about your sister."

"Enough to give up everything? Quit Hollywood? Move to the farm? She won't leave this place, you know. You'd have to move here for whatever it is you two are doing to have a chance."

"She and I will work things out. What's between us is none of your business."

"Do you actually expect me to believe that someone like you can curb his carnal appetites for months on end while my dear, darling sister stays here to play with the cows?" Gone was Levi's drawl if just for the moment. But the crudeness remained. "Do you really think you won't be tempted by all of the Hollywood tail that throws itself at you on a daily basis?"

"I said I'm nothing like you," Colton spit.

"Well, the magazines must have been wrong about you for all of these years, then, playboy." Levi was baiting him.

When he didn't bite, when he didn't take a swing, Haven's brother pulled a stack of papers out of his jacket pocket. Then he threw them unceremoniously on the ground.

He couldn't have made them land in a more perfect arrangement if he had tried. Before Haven, all manner of Colton's sins had been laid out for her to see.

Sure, she knew what he'd done, enough of it anyway. But to see it with her own eyes? Him, obviously staring down a girl's blouse as he reached up under the back of her sparkling silver miniskirt, just for a second. Him, leaning over a line of drugs, dollar bill in hand, eyes already bloodshot. Him, swigging from a liter of whiskey, pouring the brown liquid down his throat as though he'd only recently finished crossing a desert and the bottle was full of life-giving water. Him, passed out on the floor as Moira attempted to revive him.

The last incident, the evidence of which was at the top of the pile, had been the one that had spurred Moira to make arrangements for him to attend rehab. Colton had almost died. He'd never known that a picture of his close call had circulated its way through the intricate trails of the Internet.

"Haven, please," Colton said, reaching out.

But her eyes were transfixed. All she could see were his transgressions.

A wolf in sheep's clothing.

Levi had done his job well. He'd made it look as though he had come to save his sister from Colton. Not the other way around.

Colton tried to reach for Haven again, but she pulled away.

"Don't touch me," she said, then turned to her brother. "Levi, let's go."

Haven walked out of the barn with her brother in tow. Colton couldn't bear to turn around. He was afraid he'd see Levi's smug face and be forced to kill him.

As soon as he was sure that they were back in the main house, Colton headed for the bunkhouse. He grabbed his cell phone, threw it on the charger, and waited for it to revive enough to be able to make a call.

"Colton? Is that you?" Moira asked.

"Yes."

"Did you tell her?"

"Yes."

"How did it go?"

"She won't speak to me."

"Did you tell her about the farm?"

"I only got as far as saying Levi had taken out a loan."

"She doesn't know he's planning to sell the place, then?"

"No. She doesn't."

"What happened? Why didn't you tell her?"

"Levi is what happened. He presented her with photographic proof of all of my sins."

"What?"

"He printed out a stack of compromising pictures of me from the Internet."

"But she already knows what you've done, what your problems are."

"It's different seeing the evidence. You know that. She and I had just kissed. I told her I loved her."

"Wait. You told her you loved her?"

"Yes."

"What did she say?"

"The first time I said it, she only responded with the fact that she cared about me. The second time…"

But there hadn't been a second time. He had been thinking it, had been yelling it at her in his mind when Levi was painting him to be the devil himself. But he'd never actually said it. He'd only told her over and over again how much he wanted her.

"Moira?"

"Yes."

147

"I have to go."

"But Colton…"

"I'll call you in a little bit. I promise. Right now, I have to speak to Haven."

Colton tossed his cell phone closer to the jack so it could continue to charge. Then he headed out of the bunkhouse door toward the main residence. The screen door slammed behind him as he extended his stride. He arrived at the entrance to Haven's home before he figured out what he was going to say.

Nevertheless, he yanked open the screen door and darted into the kitchen. It was where Haven would be.

Sure enough, there she was, making dinner for her creep of a brother.

"Mr. Grey. Nice of you to join us," Levi drawled.

"Cut the crap, Levi. I'm not here to talk to you. I'm here to talk to your sister. Haven," Colton added, looking at her. "Please. Come with me."

He stretched out his hand, but she didn't reach for it.

"Haven. You know me," Colton implored.

She couldn't look at him, but she followed him out the door.

"Don't be a fool, baby sister. He will break your heart."

But Levi's heart wasn't in the warning. He had turned his attention to the chili Haven was making for them to eat for dinner.

Colton eventually took her by the hand and led her to a giant oak that would block them from Levi's view.

"Haven, I'm sorry," Colton began. "I wish I'd never done any of those things. If I had known you before, I never would have."

"Colton. You don't need to apologize. That was your life."

"I saw the horror in your eyes, Haven. I know how those pictures made you feel."

She looked off into the distance at one of the nearby fields. She couldn't deny it. Those pictures had hurt her. It was apparent on her face. They were hurting her still.

"I'm not that guy anymore," he promised.

"Colton, don't," Haven protested.

"It's true. I'm different."

"Colton, please. This is all too much."

"I love you, Haven. Can't you see that? I love you."

Her eyes were brimming with tears.

"I love you."

She broke into a sob then.

Quickly, he lowered his tone, decreasing his intensity. "Why are you crying?"

"Because love has never been enough," she confessed. The tears fell even faster. "Love is never enough," she repeated.

Colton could see it now, her life playing out before his eyes. Everyone she had ever loved had hurt her in some way. Some because they could, others because they couldn't help it. Love wasn't a sanctuary for Haven. It was a prison. It kept her caged. It had never set her free.

"Haven. Listen to me. You don't owe me anything. You can choose to do whatever you want. I don't expect anything from you. I just want you to know that I love you."

She looked up at him.

"I love you," he said again, resting his forehead on hers.

When she didn't pull back or protest, he repeated his declaration.

"I will always love you," he whispered against her ear.

Just one more time.

"I love you," he said, confirming his pledge.

She continued to cry, burrowing into him, letting out all of the pain. As she did this, he pulled her even further into his arms.

"I love you," he said, breaking his vow to stop repeating the obvious.

Slowly, Haven accepted his embrace.

He'd reached her. Despite Levi, despite his own fears, despite Haven's reticence, he'd reached her.

"I'll pay off the loan," he said. "Don't worry."

She said nothing.

"And I won't let him sell the farm."

Haven coughed, then took a step back.

"What?"

"I said I won't let him sell the farm."

He realized his mistake too late. He hadn't yet told her Levi had put the farm up for sale.

"Why would you need to stop him from selling it?"

"Levi's put it on the market."

"He can't…"

"He can, love. And he did."

All of the life drained out of her. Colton couldn't imagine what it must feel like to have the thing that you had fought so hard to prevent coming at you faster than you could ever have imagined. But Haven was living that now.

Her pain was so consuming that she hadn't so much as flinched when Colton had called her *love*. And Colton was so caught up in holding her and thinking about the many ways he could harm Levi that he hadn't noticed when her tears had subsided.

"I'm okay," she finally said.

"You sure?" He wiped a stray tear from her cheek.

"Yes." After a minute, she asked, "Colton?"

"Uh-huh," he murmured, looking down at her.

"Can I stay with you tonight?"

"You can stay with me always," he promised.

And he knew it was true. He would never get tired of this girl. It was impossible. Her big heart, her warm spirit. She was worth a thousand of him.

Chapter Thirty

Yet Haven enjoyed being with Colton, found comfort in his presence.

Almost as if to confirm this, she took his hand and led him in the direction of the bunkhouse. As they got closer, he started to pull her toward the place he'd been sleeping since his arrival. But she shook her head, leading him past.

"No. I'm taking you somewhere else," she said.

When he threatened to stop, she turned to him and said, "You promised I could stay with you."

The implication that he would be breaking his pledge to be there for her, to comfort her, if he didn't go along with her apparent plan, drained the fight from him.

He didn't have it in him to argue. Not anymore. She could have any part of him she wanted if that was what she needed to weather the storm that her life had become.

Still, the sight of the chicken coop caused him to balk.

"I know I said I love you, Haven," he started, "but I'm not ready to conquer my fear of chickens to prove it."

"One of the buildings is empty," she confessed. "That's where we're headed."

"I hate to be a drag, but I'm going to require proof

before I step inside."

"There's a flashlight stashed nearby. I'll grab it and show you I'm not lying."

True to her word, she did. So he followed her in.

Once inside, she led him up a set of stairs to a small loft. It was enclosed and must have functioned as an office at some point. Probably after the chickens were cleared out. Otherwise, the stench would have been awful. The rest of the structure was empty.

"We use this building for storage when the rest of our harvest barns are full."

Colton didn't reply. His heart was beating fast.

Her body language had shifted. Her voice was softer. She wasn't going to give him time to ease into this. She wasn't going to allow him the chance to second-guess their timing yet again.

No. When she turned around, she didn't smile shyly, she didn't fidget with her hands and stare at the floor, she didn't prolong the inevitable. Instead, she kissed him.

Her kiss was soft, tender. It spoke of her goodness and her trust.

Colton didn't resist. He couldn't. He kissed her back. Mimicking her movements. He allowed her to set the pace. He didn't deepen the kiss, didn't change anything, just enjoyed the moment.

After a time, her hands began to roam over his body. Up his back they traced. Down his back they trailed. Colton was careful not to allow his fingertips the same freedom. Not now, not yet.

His hands were light upon her frame. They didn't ask anything of her. They just cradled her, holding her close to him. But not crushing her with his desire.

For what felt like hours, Haven traced the edges of his skin. She appeared to be trying to memorize the swell and fall of his muscles with her fingertips. Her touch was soft, yet firm. Her energy coursed into him at the places where their skin met.

More than once, a sound of longing escaped from Colton. And each time it did, Haven would smile against his lips, happy that she could cause such wanting in him.

Just when Colton thought he would die from his wanting, when he was beginning to believe it was possible for a human being to spontaneously combust, she paused her kisses and took a step back.

With asking in her eyes, she slowly began to unbutton her shirt. This shirt was dry. She had changed from the one she had had on in the barn.

Underneath her shirt was a white tank top. And beneath that, a white bra.

Colton couldn't help himself. He kissed her again, then rested his forehead against hers. Being separated from her was too much. And anticipating being closer to her was even more torturous. She smiled as she returned his kiss. Then she took a small step back once more.

Colton's heartbeat quickened as she stared at him expectantly. With a slight gesture of her hand, she signaled him to catch up. She wanted him to remove his shirt, too.

"I don't have—" he began. He had to be practical. There was only so much that he could risk with her.

Haven pointed to the side table near the far wall where a handful of shiny silver foil packages rested. She had planned this. Maybe not tonight. But at some point, she had thought about bringing him here.

"And you're sure?" he asked, eyeing the bed.

His body was yelling at him, ordering him to stop finding excuses, to stop finding reasons this night couldn't happen. The cells that made up his being couldn't take even a second more of hesitation.

When Haven nodded her head, signaled that she was sure, he pulled his shirt off over his head.

Both of their eyes darkened with desire. He could feel his eyelids becoming heavy, taking on the literal visage of the bedroom eyes he was known for. Haven's eyes, too, were weighted with the feelings swirling in her body.

As soon as Colton was sure that he could move at an acceptable pace, remain gentle, be the man that Haven deserved at this moment, he took a step closer. Taking her face in his hands, he bent down, pressing his lips to hers. His kisses were as sweet as those she had offered him only moments ago.

"Haven," he whispered, pulling back, "you are beautiful."

She smiled at his words.

"The most beautiful person I have ever met," he breathed. His entire being was saturated with wanting. "I love you. I truly do."

Her eyes misted. "I love you, too," she whispered.

Her words were air to a drowning man.

Chapter Thirty-One

Colton pulled Haven closer to him. Her hands hadn't left his chest since he took off his shirt. She caressed him as she stared.

"You're beautiful, too."

"Not as beautiful as you," he leaned down and whispered in her ear.

He wanted her to be comfortable. Despite his desire, he didn't wish to rush this, to rush her.

At his words, she reached behind her back and undid her bra. She covered herself as she removed the straps and tossed the undergarment to the floor.

"We don't have to," Colton said.

"No. I want this. I'm just a little shy."

"Would it help if I turned around?"

"I don't think so." Haven looked at the ground. "But could you close your eyes? Just for a bit?"

"Sure," he said, obeying her soft command. He could hear the rustle of fabric. His mind cursed itself for missing the unveiling. Watching a woman fully undress for the first time was as tantalizing an experience as could ever be had. With Haven, it would have been nothing less than magical.

"I'm done," she said.

Colton opened his eyes to see Haven standing naked before him. She was more breathtaking than his overactive imagination could have guessed. Her curves were perfection, her edges inviting.

Colton couldn't hide his response. Haven refused to look, but she must have noticed because she started to blush even more.

"You're perfect," he breathed.

She rushed into his arms then. Her bravery extinguished.

Colton kissed her forehead. Then each of her cheeks. Then her nose, then her chin, and finally her mouth.

When he felt her relax in his arms, he began kissing her neck. She moved her head to the side to provide him with better access.

As he kissed her, he could feel her hands at the waistband of his jeans. Once or twice, her fingers traced the skin running along the top edge of the band. It was amazing how much fire a few inches of skin could create.

When she reached for his button, he pulled back. "I want to go slow," he said.

She responded by kissing him.

He pulled back once more. "I don't want to hurt you," he urged.

"You would never hurt me," she said, moving her mouth closer to his lips.

"I would never hurt you on purpose," he answered. "But this is your first time."

"I trust you," she replied.

And he could see in her eyes that she did. That alone would make him go slow no matter what she did. "Okay," he answered, and she slowly unzipped his pants.

As she was tugging down his jeans, the denim got

stuck, stalling around his hips. He wanted to laugh at the look of disappointment on her face. Instead, he helped her, tugging the offending fabric free and tossing his pants to the side.

Once in just his underwear, he kissed her again. His hands gently traced the angles of her face before burying themselves in her hair.

She copied the movements of his mouth, threading her fingers through his hair as well. When she tugged once more at the back of his neck, he responded immediately by deepening the kiss.

Her mouth tasted sweet. It was all that existed in the universe.

Just as he thought he might pass out from the pleasure, she asked, "Should we go to the bed?"

The bed was next to the nightstand. On the nightstand was what they needed if this night was to continue in the direction it was headed.

"Yes," he answered, his voice low in his throat.

Her soft hand led him to where they were going. He should have been the one leading her.

Haven crawled onto the bed and slid underneath the covers. Colton faced the wall, removed his underwear, and outfitted himself with the necessary supplies.

Then he quickly slid under the sheet until his skin was once again touching hers. He kissed her mouth. Then her shoulder. Then he descended even lower.

Haven guided his mouth back with the pressure of a single finger beneath his chin. "Not tonight."

He stopped all movement.

"No. I mean, I want you."

"It's okay," he said, confused. "We don't have to

go all the way."

"No. I want you. Now."

When he still didn't seem to comprehend, she said, "As in I *want you*, want you."

Colton finally understood. She didn't want any more foreplay.

When he was able to concentrate once more, he took a deep breath to steady his nerves. It had been a long time since he'd been nervous doing this. With Haven, everything was different. In some ways, this was his first time as well.

Satisfied that he could proceed without losing total control, Colton guided himself over her. As desire sparked in her eyes, he hesitated for only a second. He wanted to remember the way she looked now. Always.

Certain that he'd committed the image to memory, he carefully joined their bodies, willing the moment to be as painless for Haven as possible.

When she didn't protest, when all he could see was the wanting left in her eyes, he began to move. He was careful to make sure that he was supporting the majority of his weight, so she didn't feel any burden.

Haven's eyes burned as he stared at her, taking in everything she was willing to show him.

With little effort, they found their rhythm. They were meant for each other at the deepest level.

Colton whispered every compliment he could think of in her ear.

Haven absorbed his words as she did his energy.

When he wasn't whispering to her, Colton was kissing her. And Haven was kissing him back. Her lips were perfection, her ministrations a balm to his soul. For a brief second, Colton was pulled from the bliss of being with Haven in this way by worry about what would follow.

Noting this, Haven wiped the concern from his brow with her thumb. "I'm okay," she whispered in his ear. "I'll be okay."

He nodded his head, not quite believing her.

When she repeated that she was more than fine, that she was in fact enraptured, he gave in. Colton devoted himself to the task of pleasing her. It wasn't a totally selfless act. With each ounce of pleasure he created for her, he was paid in kind. Being with Haven was like flying. There were no boundaries. There were no words. There was only the sensation of total blissful freedom.

As the tension built to the point that it had to break, Colton summoned the will to keep himself in check. He would see Haven through to her crescendo before he sampled what he knew was coming.

"I'm..." she tried to warn, then shivered uncontrollably beneath him.

As she released herself into him, he did the same, happy, for once, to let himself go. White light sparked at the corner of his vision as a celestial feeling overtook him.

"That was the most...amazing..." she breathed a moment later. Her panting stymied her sentence.

"That was you," he confirmed, pressing his lips to hers.

"Can we...?" she asked, speaking around his mouth.

He smiled into her lips. "Yes," he said. "As many times as you want."

No man in his right mind would ever deny himself

and the one he loved entrance to a heaven like that. Not ever.

Chapter Thirty-Two

Colton woke to find Haven still sleeping beside him. Her shoulders rose and fell with each one of her breaths. Watching her sleep was in itself rapturous. It was as though her lungs were making music only he could hear; her face was transmitting a feeling only he could feel. He could watch her sleep for hours.

But he had things he wanted to do before she woke up.

He had to help her. He had to make arrangements with Levi. It was clear that Haven's ne'er-do-well brother had come back to the farm because he knew he could catch a big fish in Colton. Perhaps he had only sought to sell some information about the once-ailing star prior to his arrival. But upon seeing Colton's feelings for his sister, Levi must have decided that he could secure a payday that would set him up for a while if he played his cards right.

Quietly, Colton slipped out of bed. He was silent as he picked up the pieces of his clothing that were strewn about the loft.

If Colton was right, if Levi wanted a share of his money, he would give it to him.

Haven couldn't lose her farm. It was who she was.

And Colton knew a thing or two about losing your way.

Haven wouldn't be able to take the blow. Her heart

would be ripped from her chest. It was a tragedy he couldn't bear to watch. She didn't deserve to suffer such pain.

As he descended the stairs, he heard a soft question emanating from underneath the covers. "Where are you going?"

"Shh. Nowhere," he answered. "Go back to bed."

She started to get up.

"Wait," he called, returning to the bed they had shared last night.

At her request, he lay down beside her.

He didn't want her following him. He had to make his arrangements with Levi in private. Haven wouldn't let him do what he planned on doing.

Colton held her until he was sure she had fallen back to sleep. Once her sleep had deepened and he could be assured the chance to slip away, he slid his arms from around her body and set off to find Levi once more.

At the main house, Colton discovered Levi sitting on the couch with a few bags of chips, a jar of peanut butter with a spoon sticking out of it, and a dozen empty soda cans littered about him. The man was a pig.

"Mornin'," Levi greeted in a way that made Colton's skin crawl. His smirk was palpable in his tone.

"Good morning."

"You have a fun night with my sister?"

Colton balled his hands into fists. If it wouldn't harm the deal, he'd take a swing at Levi. Right here and right now. His knuckles were itching to connect with the creep's face.

"Relax, lover boy," Levi responded. "I'm only giving you a hard time. What Haven does is up to her."

"So, you only play the loving brother when she is around, then?"

"You and I both know what I am. We're from the same breed. No need to keep the pretense up with a fellow professional liar. I'm not method."

"I act for a living, Levi. I don't put on a daily show for everyone I know."

"The tabloids tell a different story."

"Look. I know you don't want Haven to be with me—"

"I don't care who Haven is with. But it does help that you want to fight so hard for her. Makes getting what I want easier."

"And what exactly is that?" Colton was going to make him say it.

"You've come to offer to buy the farm, haven't you?"

Colton hated that Levi was as good as he was at manipulating people. "So, you aren't here to play her, then?" Again, he wanted confirmation straight from the snake's lips.

"No, lover boy. I'm here to play you."

"You make me sick." He wished he could say he was surprised. But he'd expected as much.

"They all say that eventually," Levi drawled. "But I can deal with losing your good opinion. A nice bachelor's pad in Malibu will soften the blow."

"How much do you want?"

"Twice what the place is worth. Twenty million."

"I can't just write a check for twenty million. I don't have that much in liquid assets."

"Well, you better figure something out, then. I have another buyer interested in my sale price of eight million."

"You are the most disgusting human being to ever have—" Colton said, advancing on Levi.

"Colton?" Haven asked. "What's going on?"

Colton immediately dropped his raised fists. He was about to hit Haven's brother. He was. He couldn't deny it. And such an act would have only driven up the asking price for the place, suiting Levi's intentions just fine.

Before Colton could formulate a response, Haven's brother jumped in. "I was helping him prepare for a part. He needed to go over his idea for a fight scene."

"I thought they paid choreographers for that kind of stuff?" she asked skeptically.

"Colton's million-dollar ideas are how he earns the big bucks, love."

At Levi's use of the word *love*, Colton had to do everything in his power not to finish what he had started. Mongrels like Levi didn't deserve to address girls like Haven with the word *love* even if only in a brotherly way.

Instead, Colton turned to Haven, walked over to her, whispered in her ear that he was going to get started on the chores, and kissed her on the cheek. "I'll see you for lunch," he said.

"Good talk," Levi called after him.

Colton headed to the bunkhouse to grab his cell, then found a place tucked away behind a cluster of trees. He called Moira. "Moira, listen. I need your help."

The message he recorded on her voicemail sounded desperate. He was desperate. She would call him back as soon as she got it. He just hoped she would get it in time.

Colton had a feeling. The longer he took to acquire the money, the more Levi would ask for the family farm. And twenty million dollars was more than a bit of a stretch.

Still, Colton couldn't stand the idea of Haven's Eden belonging to anyone other than her.

Moira, he thought. *Please call me back as soon as you get my message. I need your help.*

Then he headed off to do the chores he had said he would do, cell phone tucked discreetly into the side pocket of his jeans, his mind on a million things all at once.

Chapter Thirty-Three

With a bale of hay held over his head, Colton finally got the call he had been expecting. Quickly, he dropped the bound flakes and answered his cell. "Moira. I'm so glad you called."

"Colton. I don't have much time. What's up?"

"Levi has offered me a chance to buy the farm."

"I'd say that's great, but I have a feeling there is a catch."

"There is. He wants twenty million for the place."

"Colton, it's barely worth ten. Nobody would pay that much."

"He will sell it for eight to anyone other than me."

"I see," Moira responded.

Colton could sense that her allegiances were being pulled in different directions. He wanted to tell her it was no use, that nothing she could think of would get him to change his mind. Instead, he waited for her to formulate what she wanted to say, then politely listened until she was finished.

"Colton, as Haven's cousin and someone who loves her a great deal, I want nothing more than to have you liquidate everything you own and buy the place. But as your publicist and someone who well knows that you can't really afford to do this, I have to tell you to let him sell the farm."

"Are you finished?"

"Only if you are taking what I've just said seriously."

"I've heard you, Moira. I have. But it's her parents' place. Was her parents' place. She loves it here."

"Colton. Haven needs to move on. Her whole life is attached to that farm."

"That's why I can't let Levi take it away from her."

"That's why it has to go. She will never find anyone who can live there with her, who will love that place as much as she does. Farming isn't as lucrative as it once was. Owning it won't be enough. She'll have to have money to invest in repairs, to buy equipment, pay seasonal workers. The farm will never make back what it needs to."

"I can't believe what you're saying—"

"I know. Trust me, I do. I never thought I'd want to see her parted from that place. I promise you, Colton. If Levi was offering it for sale for two million or four or six, I would say that we could make it work. Even eight. I would balk, but I wouldn't try to convince you to walk away from eight. But twenty? No way. Twenty million is way too much."

"Do I have it?"

"Colton, I'm not your accountant."

"Moira, you know everything there is to know about me. Do you think I have it?"

"Barely, but yes. If we get creative."

"Then contact my accountant and my attorney and have them do what is necessary."

"Colton, at least think about this."

"I've thought about it. This is what I want."

Moira hesitated before saying, "I never should have sent you out there."

"Sometimes, it's the savior that ends up needing the saving," he answered, then clicked off the phone.

Twenty million, he thought. *I'm just glad I have enough.*

Chapter Thirty-Four

"How are you feeling?" Haven asked, walking up behind him and wrapping her arms around his waist. One of the horses in a stall nearby nickered at her arrival.

He turned around to face her. "Great. How about you?" he responded.

"Colton, what's wrong? You look so…sad."

"I'm fine."

"Did your film fall through?"

"No," he answered. "Exactly the opposite."

I'll be gone far longer than I thought. The latest update from Moira had made him aware of that. Because Moira had felt guilty or because she was just that good at her job, Colton's publicist, along with his agent, had managed to secure for him several additional, supremely lucrative deals. As part of her strategy, Moira had leaked a handful of swoonworthy stories about his recovery that detailed how well he was doing and feeling now that he was on the straight and narrow. None of the pieces mentioned Haven, of course. That, they had both agreed, was off limits.

In order to obtain the above-average paydays that she was seeking and that Colton now needed, Moira had also played hardball with a few bigwigs at the larger movie studios, showing them graphs depicting exactly how much money actors tended to generate at the box office in the first few years after a comeback.

As it turned out, it was quite a bit. Colton had been shocked when he had found out just how generous America and her international compatriots were when enjoying the sight of a bad boy turning good.

Colton's agent, for her part, had sent him every script flying around Los Angeles that was looking for a leading man. The projects he had showed even the remotest interest in, she had helped Moira fight for, sticking to the game plan of demanding top dollar. Most of the ones he had truly wanted he had gotten.

A few big-name producers and directors had voiced their continued reluctance, but at the urging of Moira and his agent, they had decided to take a chance on trusting him, the promised dollar signs having surely swayed their decision more than any loyalty to a Cinderella-style tale.

"You have another project, then?" Haven asked, interrupting his train of thought.

"I have six," he answered.

"Six projects?"

"Six new projects in addition to the ones I was already contracted to star in."

"What are you saying?"

"I'm afraid," he confessed, "I won't be around much. Not at all, really."

"Surely, you'll get time off in between…"

"Moira and my agent have made sure that I will be busy for the next couple of years."

"The next couple of years? Colton, what does that mean?"

"It means, when I leave here in less than two weeks, I won't see you for the next forty-eight months."

"Forty-eight months? That's four years. You can't possibly be busy for four years."

"A lot of the filming is overseas. And I have promotions to do in between projects. I won't be able to come back here to visit."

"You won't be able to, or you don't want to?"

Her question was like a blow to the chest. He took a steadying breath, then leaned down to kiss her. He shouldn't have, but he couldn't help it.

Haven moved back, away from him, and repeated her question.

"I won't be able to, Haven. If I had my choice, I'd stay."

"You have a choice," she told him. "People always have a choice, Colton."

He sighed, running his fingers through his hair. She was going to make him lose every last strand, if only for pulling them out in moments like these.

"I, uh, I'm in a little bit of a financial pickle," he said. He had to give her something.

"Is it because you helped me out?" she asked.

Tread carefully, he warned himself. *Do not mess this up. She can't know.* "It's because of some decisions I made."

"I don't understand. I thought you were going to be set for life after your next film."

"Not after my next film, but after the franchise it's attached to ends. Yes. I was going to be," he answered, anxious for her to know he wasn't lying previously.

"Then how can things have changed so much between then and now?"

"I took a gamble," he answered. "It didn't pay off."

Haven looked at him as though he had just done

the stupidest thing she could think of. "You invested your money, and you lost it?"

"I set up an opportunity that I thought would be beneficial," he said, referencing his decision to draw Levi away from the farm by an offer of work in the movies. "It's turned out to be a bit of a money pit."

"Can't you call it off somehow? Limit the damage?"

"What's done is done," he answered.

"How much did you lose?"

"Close to everything."

"How are you going to live?" she wondered.

"The studios will pay for my food and lodging while I am working. They will cover my expenses when I am on the circuit promoting my work as well. I will only need to take care of myself a few days out of the year."

"Colton. I'm sorry. I wish there was something I could do."

"There is," he answered, taking a step closer, tracing her face with his finger. "Be happy."

She wrapped herself around him. He could feel the tears from her cheeks dropping onto his shirt.

"Please," he whispered. "Just be happy. You deserve it."

Chapter Thirty-Five

"Is it done?" Colton asked Moira, who was tapping a pen maniacally at the other end of the line.

"Yes, Mr. Grey," she answered because she was in front of others.

"And the clause? It's in there?"

"It is." After she excused herself and slipped into another room, she elaborated. "He gets fifteen million. The rest goes to Haven in a trust that I can use to help her keep the farm going."

"How did you bargain him down?"

"I threatened to blacklist him in the industry."

"So he wants fame as much as money, then?" Colton would have chuckled if the circumstances weren't so dire.

"Colton, I'm sorry. I can't help but think this is all my fault."

"It isn't, Moira. You helped me get sober. Haven helped me get sober. Without both of you, I would have blown through my savings anyway. At least, this way, it goes to something real, something worthwhile."

"I think, if you told her—"

"She can't know anything. We agreed." When his publicist didn't respond, he added, "You promised, Moira."

"I know. I know. I just don't like her thinking that you are up and leaving her for no good reason."

"It's what she must think. So she can move on."

"I could talk her into visiting you."

"Haven doesn't belong in my world. She deserves to be someplace where people and places are real. I don't want her wholesomeness corrupted. I won't be the thing that ruins her…" Colton could barely get out the words.

"Does she know?"

"Know what?" He was perplexed. They had just gone over the fact that Haven would never know—no, could never know—what he'd done for her financially.

"Does she know you love her?" Moira repeated as though she was talking to a simpleton.

"Yes. I've told her. Too many times."

"She may wait for you."

"That's not what I want."

"You are a good guy, Colton."

"No. I am a reformed bad guy. There is a difference."

Moira chuckled. "I shouldn't laugh," she added.

"No. Please do. Someone should. Other than Levi."

"He'll get his," Moira said emphatically.

"Yes. He probably will. But I can't wish for that. Not when I know how much it will hurt Haven." Colton sighed.

"Listen, Colton. I hate to do this, but I've got to go. I am sure it is hard to imagine, but yours is only the second biggest pickle one of my clients has found themselves in this week."

"A dead body, then, is it?"

"More like too many bodies. In the same bed. At the same time."

"Crossing gender lines?"

175

"Crossing every line."

"They don't pay you the big bucks for nothing."

"Very funny." She laughed. "I'll see you in a couple of days, okay? Hang in there?"

"I will, Moira. See you then." Then Colton hung up the phone.

He hated Levi. Because of him, Haven would think he was returning never to come back, not because he had to so he could pay off the loans he'd taken out against future salaries, but because he wanted to leave.

If he could have had his lawyer put a clause in the contract stating that Levi would have to kill himself after he was done spending all of the money he'd received from the sale of the farm, he might have. Except to have done so would end up hurting Haven.

And that was the problem with love. At some point, you'd do anything to protect the one to whom you were devoted. Even it meant burning down your figurative house while you were still standing in it.

Chapter Thirty-Six

Colton found Haven crying in the barn the next day.

"What's wrong?" he asked, rushing over to stand by her. She was just outside of Cicero's stall.

"It's Levi."

He's gone, Colton thought.

"He left," she confirmed. "In the middle of the night."

Colton took her in his arms. He couldn't say he was sorry that Levi was gone. But he was sorry that his departure was causing Haven so much pain. "It will be okay. It will all be okay."

"No. It won't. He still has power of attorney over Mom. I didn't get a chance to talk to him about signing her over."

"It's taken care of."

"What do you mean 'it's taken care of'?" she questioned, looking up at him.

"I spoke with Moira. She convinced Levi that it would be best if you could make all of your mother's medical decisions."

"Oh."

"She'll send you the paperwork."

"Oh."

"And he can't sell the farm. Not anymore. It's been put into your name."

What Colton didn't tell Haven was that her brother would never fully come back into her life again, not if he wanted to hang onto the bulk of the money from the sale of the farm. It was in the contract. That part Colton himself had thought to include. Levi could visit Haven on a select few major holidays, but only when others were around to protect her from any more of his potential schemes.

Colton wasn't the only one who would remain mum on the subject either. Levi couldn't tell Haven about the clause. Or the sale of the farm. Or any of the worst of the things that he had done. Built into the deal that he had signed was a very strict set of confidentiality agreements. Levi may have arrived armed with a talent for manipulating people, but Colton had spent his formative years growing up in the epicenter of the cultural scene of Los Angeles, in the movie business, the profession that had invented the never-ending list of contractual clauses and witnessed guarantees.

Colton was more than just a pretty face. And he was determined to protect the girl he loved.

It hadn't hurt that Colton's lawyer was the head of one of the best legal teams in existence. One accustomed to getting the rich and famous out of far trickier situations than the one Colton had recently found himself mired in.

In truth, he had thought about driving down the price of the farm. But he'd decided to work on giving Haven some of the money instead. No matter what happened between them, investing in her was the best bet he could make. He wanted to know she'd be okay if, or more likely when, he wasn't around.

The thought of her settling down with someone else was painful. But she deserved better anyway. As he had told Moira, Colton knew he was not a good man, just a reformed bad one.

Levi had at least been right about that.

"Colton, why are you being so quiet?"

Because I don't want to leave you, he thought. *And because I do. For your own good.* "I'm sorry," he said instead. "I was just thinking about the future."

"Moira is supposed to get in tomorrow?"

"Yes. We leave the next day."

"So, we have the farm to ourselves tonight?"

He nodded. He knew what she was thinking. They hadn't spent an evening alone together since the night they had stayed in the loft. Tonight, however, they'd have the opportunity with no potential interruptions looming on the horizon.

Colton wanted more than anything to be with Haven one last time. But he wasn't sure he could handle it. He would know, after all, that it would be the last time that they would ever be in each other's arms while she looked at him with hopeful eyes, willing him to rearrange his commitments so he could change their future, make more room in his life for her.

But Colton couldn't. Absolutely zero wiggle room existed in the deals he had signed. The contracts were ironclad. Each missed day or delayed call would cost him money and not just small sums. He needed every cent he could get to survive right now, not just to set up an early retirement. And once the money was coming in, he wanted to earn enough to never have to be in the position that he was in now ever again. Considering how fickle the movie business was and the fact that he had almost fallen out of favor with those in charge of directing and producing the pictures that made it to the silver screen, he needed to do as much work as he could for as long as he could so he might, one day, be able to call all of the shots in his life once more.

Maybe then... he wondered. But it wasn't fair to ask Haven to wait. Or to leave the place she loved most in the world.

"What do you think?" she asked.

It was only then that he realized he hadn't been listening. "I'm sorry," he admitted. "I didn't catch the last part."

"I was saying I could make dinner, and we could eat on a blanket under the stars. What do you think?"

"I think that sounds lovely," he responded, kissing the top of her head. "Just the kind of night we both need."

Haven leaned up to kiss him on the cheek, then headed off to do some chores.

They had it down to a science now. She took care of whatever he wasn't skilled enough to do or whatever he was unwilling to do, i.e., tend to the chickens, while he did the things he couldn't possibly screw up, such as shovel manure.

A few stalls mucked clean later, Colton received a text from Moira.

I never said thank you, she typed.

You didn't need to, he answered back.

Being lucky enough to have met Haven was worth more than any money he could ever have accumulated in the bank.

The tug at his chest when he thought this told him to drop what he was doing now, so he could soak up every last second he could in her presence. But then she would know. As far as she was concerned, he would work something out with his schedule. Or Moira would.

Haven didn't know that he knew she'd been calling and texting Moira, trying to convince her to get Colton a few weeks off here or a month off there.

True to her word, Moira had said nothing about what had gone down since Levi had put the farm up for sale. Not a single thing for over a month.

Moira had assured him that she hadn't promised Haven anything, but she also hadn't told her the reasons her requests could never be met either, which, as it turned out, was just enough to keep Haven going.

Colton cursed himself for having to keep secrets from her. He felt as though this whole sordid situation was his fault. Like he could have protected her better, like he should have. Regardless of the circumstances, good-byes had never been his strength.

This was always going to be hard.

A few more mucked stalls, a dozen filled water buckets, a swept clean walkway, a plethora of unloaded hay, a selection of stacked feedbags, and a few equine baths later, the horses and their barn were squared away.

From there, Colton proceeded to tend to the handful of cows that had been brought up for monitoring. One appeared to be lame. The others had a bit of rain rot on their backs. They required a little TLC before being turned back into the veritable wild. So, he put liniment on the cow that needed liniment and a sulfur-based paste on those suffering from rain rot.

By the time he was done doing what needed to be done, Colton was dog-tired. Nevertheless, he tried desperately to think of something else that he could use to postpone the evening ahead. Nothing came to him. No matter how creative he got, everything he thought of was already done.

When, finally, he was forced to accept that there wasn't anything left to invent to do, Colton reluctantly headed back to the bunkhouse. He needed a shower and some time to think if he was going to survive the night ahead. It was true that he wanted to find a way out of the stargazing that was on the evening's menu, but he knew, in the depth of his bones, that there was nothing he could do to release himself from the lover's picnic that Haven had planned.

Despite the fact that, the more he thought about it, the worse an idea it seemed to be, he knew she was unlikely to budge. There was nothing he could say to convince her that spending the night together wasn't essential.

Her mind was still on beginnings after all, trying to secure ways to see him as often as possible. He was the only one who knew that the night ahead was a farewell, not a hello.

No. There was no chance that Colton could convince her to spend the evening away from his company. And also none that he would survive intact. Just imagining their good-bye was excruciating. Having to live through it, knowing she was in the dark, would be deadly. The Colton going into this night would not be the same as the Colton coming out of it. Not by a long shot.

Chapter Thirty-Seven

"You look nice," Haven offered as Colton walked into the main house's kitchen.

Predictably, Haven was throwing some food items together into clear plastic containers and placing them in a picnic basket.

"Not as nice as you," he countered.

Despite the futility of the endeavor, he'd tried to come up with an excuse not to come. He'd gone through every possible reason he could think of to keep himself from meeting her. He'd started to pretend to be sick. Hell, he'd started to pretend to have leprosy. But in the end, he hadn't been able to force himself to break her heart a moment earlier then he had to.

"I'm just about ready," she said as she grabbed two glasses and what looked like a bottle of wine.

"A little young to be drinking, aren't you, Ms. Morrow?"

She smiled. "If I am old enough to run a farm, I am old enough to drink."

He chuckled.

"But this is only sparkling grape juice."

"Sounds nice," he responded.

"I thought so." She smiled.

"You need some help?" Colton asked.

"You can grab the blankets out of the hall closet."

"Which ones?"

"They're both dark blue."

"Got it," he responded.

Luckily, they were the only two dark blue blankets in the cupboard. And they had clearly been outside more than once, leaving zero doubt that they were the blankets to which she was referring.

"You have a thing for picnics?" he asked as they headed out of the main house and into the night.

"Levi and I used to stargaze when we were younger."

Colton bristled at the name.

"Don't worry. Tonight is not a night for wondering why things aren't different. It's a night for appreciating what is."

Once more, she was playing the tune that belonged to his heartstrings alone. She amazed him with each passing second in the way that only she could do.

"I was thinking. If you wanted, you could come to one of my premieres or something."

"That's funny," she responded, laughing to herself.

"What makes it funny?" he questioned.

"Moira said the exact same thing."

"Oh. Right. I guess I forgot to tell you. She sort of knew…"

"About us? Yes. I know. I told her."

"You told her?"

"Yeah. I asked her if it would be all right to date you?"

"What on earth would make you ask for her permission?"

"I didn't want her to lose a client…if…uh…things didn't work out."

"I'm not like that," Colton assured.

"She said as much," Haven confirmed.

Colton smiled. He imagined Moira would have called Haven a total idiot for thinking such a thing. Then warned her about the stupidity of dating Hollywood men. Then offered her congratulations. That was how Moira worked.

"May I ask how long ago you asked her?" Colton asked.

"I'd rather not say."

So, before the first time she had thrown herself at him then. Moira had known about the feelings brewing between them all along. That was probably how she knew about their first kiss. Being so familiar with each of them and having been told by Haven about her interest in Colton, Moira had guessed they had kissed when they did. It was Colton's response that had confirmed her suspicions.

She keeps secrets from everybody, Colton thought, reviewing everything Moira must have been holding inside. *Even me.*

"So, what's for dinner?" he asked, when he was done reviewing his relationship with Haven from Moira's assumed perspective.

"Cheese. Cherries. Sparkling grape juice. But you already knew that. Steak sandwiches. And a surprise for dessert."

Colton stared at the ground as he walked. Such a romantic meal. Such an unworthy person to waste it on. "Haven, I'm not sure…"

"Colton. Don't argue. I can feel your hesitation in everything you do. But I'm fine, okay? I'm a big girl. If this ends, it ends. I can handle it."

"I don't think you understand."

185

"Please. I just want tonight. One normal night to be with my boyfriend."

She'd taken to calling him her boyfriend. *Great.* The lump in Colton's throat settled itself further in. He could barely swallow.

Noting his discomfort, Haven reached back and took his hand. "Please?" she asked. "Just this one night. Let me feel like a normal girl. Okay?"

"Okay," he answered because he had no other words to offer.

Chapter Thirty-Eight

Haven spread out the blankets while Colton held the basket full of food.

"There," she said, once she'd positioned a candle at each corner and lit them. The light in the jars shone brightly, making her skin look more luminescent than usual and her eyes sparkle with warmth. "Here," she said, patting the area next to her on the blanket. "Sit here."

Colton did as he was told.

"If you don't mind, you can uncork the grape juice."

"What? No screw top or home brew?"

"Very funny," she answered.

Colton grabbed the corkscrew and began uncorking the bottle. Then, he poured them each a glass of a very nonalcoholic beverage. It smelled like a little kid's juice pack.

The picnic basket Haven had was actually quite elegant. It also happened to look brand-new.

"Did you order this?" he asked, wondering where she had gotten such a nice set.

"Moira sent it a while back."

Colton vowed to kill his publicist as soon as he got the chance. For all her value when it came to industry affairs, she was really not helping with this matter at all. Maybe he could feed Moira to the lions at the San

Diego Zoo. A threatened eye for a threatened eye.

"What are you thinking?" Haven asked, taking her glass from him.

"About how to kill your cousin."

"She thought it was a nice gesture."

I am sure she did, he agreed silently to himself.

"What shall we toast to?" Haven asked.

"To your happiness," he answered.

"To our happiness," she countered, tapping her glass on his.

The empty sound of her glass touching his mimicked the sound made by his own heart. His happiness was out of the question. At least for a while.

"Colton?"

"Yes," he murmured.

"Remember what I said. We are supposed to be appreciating tonight."

"Right," he answered. "Sure thing. Operation Appreciate Tonight is a go."

Haven laughed at his silliness, then popped a Rainier cherry into her mouth. When he refused to begin eating himself, she popped one into his as well.

Snuggling close, she asked, "Tell me about the projects you will be doing."

"Haven, I don't think—"

"Come on. I want to hear."

"I thought cinema wasn't your thing."

"You may have changed my mind," she answered, nestling herself further into him.

"Okay. The first project you already know about. It's a big-budget action film with tons of special effects."

"Yes. That one Moira told me about."

"Just how often do you talk to Moira about me?"

"Almost every day."

"You call her almost every day?"

"Mostly, we text."

"Why so often?"

"At first, I was just assuring her that you were still sober."

"And now?"

"I force her to tell me as much as she will about you."

"Why?" Colton wondered.

"Because you don't talk much about yourself."

"That's not true."

"It is. You joke. You make wisecracks. But I have to fight for every real piece of information you give me about yourself."

"I've answered every question you've asked."

"You've responded to nearly every question I've posed. There is a difference."

Colton smiled into her hair. "Okay," he conceded. "I won't argue. I don't want to ruin our midnight picnic."

"'Our midnight picnic.' I like that. Maybe you can make a movie about it someday."

Colton smiled.

"Will you be making any romances?" Haven asked.

But it wasn't like when Anna used to grill him way back when, when she was going on tour and his schedule forced them to be apart. She had wanted to know if he would have access to any more pretty young things.

Haven seemed to be asking for an entirely different

reason.

"No," Colton responded. "No romances."

He had forced Moira to agree that she wouldn't sign him up for any romantic comedies, anything romantic at all. A couple of films he was now slated to appear in had a hint of a relationship between the hero and heroine, but nothing over the top. Innocent flirtation, really. The rest involved some James-Bond-style meaningless sex.

"Why not?" Haven asked. "Don't you like romances?"

He couldn't answer that question. Not without giving everything away.

Prior to meeting her, he'd had no problem starring in a romantic movie. The more opportunities he had to make young ladies swoon, the better. They were an essential part of his growing fan base.

The truth was young women were the ones driving up the profits at box offices around the world nowadays. No matter who the leading person happened to be, guy or girl.

With reluctant boyfriends in tow, they flocked to see melodramatic teen angst whenever possible, even when they had already tasted and been disappointed by first love.

No. Prior to Haven, Colton hadn't shied away from high romantic quotients. Now, however, the mere thought made him sick.

"I've said something wrong, haven't I?" she asked.

"No. You haven't."

"Is it about Anna? Did you meet her while filming a romantic comedy or something?"

"No," Colton assured. "I didn't meet her while

filming a romantic comedy, nor have I thought about her in quite some time."

"Then what is it?"

"You know what it is," he answered.

"What?"

"I have to leave soon, Haven."

"I know," she responded. "But that doesn't have to mean that we can't—"

"Doesn't it?" he asked, looking deeply into her eyes. "You'll be here. I'll be everywhere but here. I don't think we can make it work."

"I can wait."

"No, Haven. You need someone who knows farming and animals as well as you do."

"You did just fine."

"I'm serious. You need to focus on turning things around here. And I need to make back what I lost."

"Are you saying you aren't able to wait for me?"

Colton blinked. Twice. He hadn't meant it that way. He was only thinking about her.

"If you need to have relationships while you are gone, I can learn to understand."

Colton wanted to vomit. Her niceness, her understanding, was too much for him to take. "Let's talk about something else," he begged. "Please."

"Okay," she said. "But can I ask one more question before we do?"

Colton nodded his head.

"Will you miss me?"

With that, Colton drew Haven to him and hugged her as tightly as humanly possible.

Miss you? he thought. *I won't do anything else but miss you the entire time I am away.*

Chapter Thirty-Nine

Haven told Colton about all of her plans for the farm.

She confessed to him that Moira had found some old stocks that her mom had purchased a while back, which were worth a little bit now. She was planning to use that money to buy a few pieces of new equipment.

Colton smiled as he held her, glad that her voice sounded light and airy as she spoke, very different from how it used to sound in the past, when she spoke of overdue bills and the risk of losing the farm.

"That sounds great," he said when she was done chattering. "You'll be really busy, too. You won't even know I am gone."

Ouch. Why did I say that?

"I'll miss you, too," she said, turning around in his lap so she could face him. Then, she placed her hands on either side of his face and kissed his mouth.

"Haven, I'm not sure…" he began.

"Please? As a going-away present?"

"It won't…it will only…"

But she didn't listen. She kissed him. Then, she kissed him again. She tasted of sparkling grape juice and the double-chocolate-fudge cake she had made especially for him. A recipe from one of his favorite bakeries in Los Angeles.

Moira was the only one that could have gotten her

the information she needed to duplicate the delectable dessert.

Colton vowed again to kill his publicist. Twice. Only killing her twice would do.

For right now, however, he sought solely to remember this moment. What it was like to have Haven's lips pressed to his. What it was like to place his hands on the small of her back. What it was like to have the scent of her fragrant shampoo wafting its way through the fresh country air.

"Heaven," he whispered to no one in particular.

"The name's Haven," she responded, smiling into his mouth.

"Haven is a sort of heaven, don't you think?"

She didn't answer. She just kissed him in return. After what seemed like hours, she began unbuttoning his shirt.

"Haven, please. This will only make it worse. For the both of us."

"I will regret it every day of my life if we don't do this now," she said simply.

Looking into her eyes, he knew it was the truth. "Okay." He nodded, his heart already breaking in the way a heart does when it is getting too much and too little of what it wants all at the same time. "Should we go inside?" he asked, thinking a bed might be more comfortable.

"No," she answered. "I want to be with you right here. Underneath the stars."

He allowed her to finish unbuttoning his shirt. Then he watched as she began unbuttoning her own.

"Would you like some help?" he asked in a husky voice.

"No," she answered. "I want to show you what I couldn't before."

He gulped down his anticipation. With each revealed millimeter of her skin, Colton's breathing became heavier. His eyes took on the saturated look of someone deeply in love.

When she pulled the shirt from her body, he soaked it all in. Her pale skin was beautiful. Its creamy whiteness made more obvious by the midnight-blue bra she had on.

"You match the blankets," he said, amused by the coincidence.

"The blankets match me," she responded, dropping her hands to the button on her jeans.

Slowly, Haven finished undressing. When she was completely nude, she kissed him again. There was no limit to the places she would allow him to touch. But his fingers kept finding their way back to her face. He traced her hairline, her cheekbones, her lips.

He remarked time and time again upon the beauty of her eyes as he kissed her, then kissed her some more.

By the time he and Haven made love, there was nothing left unsaid. They belonged to each other as only two souls destined to could.

The soft moans Haven made as he translated into action what his heart felt with each beat burned their way into his memory.

"Colton?" she asked, her breathing raspy, consumed by desire.

"Yes," he responded, not slowing his efforts in the slightest.

"I love you."

He smiled as he tasted her lips.

"As soon as you arrived, I knew," she continued. "I was born to love you."

"No," he countered, his own voice husky. "It is the other way around. I was born to love you."

For the rest of the evening, they would make their pledges with actions and with words. When the sun finally decided to rise, there would be nothing left unsaid. And, Colton knew, the leaving would be that much more difficult for their efforts.

Chapter Forty

"Wake up," Haven said softly.

"Hmmm?" he asked, pulling the warm body next to him closer.

"The sun will be rising soon," she pointed out. "We better get up."

"Don't tell me you have one last list of chores for me to complete before I go?"

"Not exactly," she said.

There was something about her tone that jolted him awake.

She lifted her head from his chest. "I want to show you something," she clarified. "That's all."

He nodded.

She could ask for a lung, and he'd give it to her. A kidney? She could have them both. Anything, just anything for the girl that rested atop his chest.

"Do we have to hike to this place?" he asked, holding her to him so she couldn't get up, not yet.

"Ride," she replied, smiling.

"Horses?" he asked, kissing her forehead, just because he could.

"Yes."

Haven convinced him to allow her to break away. Then she stood up and put on her clothes. Her skin was bathed by the last remaining moonlight. She was beautiful. The movie industry, with all of its special effects, had nothing on nature and what it was able to create.

"You're beautiful," he called.

"Not as beautiful as you," she answered over her shoulder.

As soon as he was able to, Colton stood up to join her. It took no small amount of effort to shake his mind from the dream image before him and convince himself to face what was coming.

Moira would arrive to collect him today. With her came all of the responsibilities he had been neglecting, the ones he had originally come to this farm to prepare himself for.

He hoped his sobriety could withstand the separation from Haven and from everything she meant.

"You coming?" Haven asked.

"Of course," he answered.

They dropped off the empty food basket and the blankets and headed out to the barn.

Colton saddled Ol' Faithful, the trusty mount he had been riding since Haven had first made him get back on a horse. Haven threw on Cicero's gear.

"Should we bring our cell phones? In case Moira gets in early?" he asked.

"I left a note for her on the door," the girl with beautiful russet hair answered. "I'd rather we not be disturbed."

Colton didn't ask any more questions. He mounted his horse and followed as Cicero and Haven trotted out of the barn.

Dawn was just breaking.

Colton stared, mesmerized as he watched Haven's hair fly out behind her. The rising sun caught each strand and made it glow. The swing of Haven's hips, backlit by the birth of morning, was something to behold. The movements of her body matched her horse's stride. This entire adventure, every second he had spent on this farm, seemed like a fairy tale, one that turned the villain into something else.

"Beautiful," he said under his breath—about Haven, about the land they both loved, about everything they'd shared.

When she finally sent Cicero into a gallop, Colton's mount followed suit. He no longer had to struggle to stay centered in the saddle. He was able to keep himself slightly above the mare's back so as not to damage her spine when she ran.

The wind against his face was a welcome reminder of just how much space there was on the acres he had helped Haven keep, just how much space her love had carved into his heart.

When Haven slowed down Cicero, Colton pulled back on the reins. He was a little out of breath. Riding was much more work than it seemed. At nearly the same time, they dismounted, walking their horses a short distance before securing them to a nearby tree.

Haven took Colton's hand and led him through some brush.

"You're not taking me out to the woods to kill me, are you?"

"No."

"Preparing to tie me up, to force me to live in a secret cabin where no one can find me?"

"No."

"Then..." but Colton didn't get a chance to finish his sentence.

Haven pushed a set of long vines to the side. Past the wall of green she held at bay was an oasis of sorts, a crystal-clear pool surrounded on all sides by trees and other brush. The trees were close enough together that the light from the sun barely seeped in. They walked into shadow.

"This is beautiful," he said.

"This is what you saved." Haven hesitated.

Does she know?

"By paying off those bills, you helped me keep this."

Haven took off her shoes, found a smooth rock to sit on, and dangled her feet in the cool water. Colton soon joined her.

"Thank you," she said when he sat down.

"It's I that should be thanking you," Colton began.

"No. You've done far more for me than anybody in my life."

"And you've changed mine."

Haven leaned her head against his chest. "In some ways, I wish I were different."

"What do you mean?" Colton asked.

"I wish it wasn't so hard for me to leave this place. I could come with you."

He'd thought the same thing many times. But, in truth, he couldn't picture her anywhere but here. "You belong here," he whispered.

"I belong with you."

After a time, he made a promise he knew he would be unable to keep. "Maybe I can cancel one of the projects."

"Moira said the contracts are ironclad."

"I should have known you would ask Moira to get

me more than a few days off here and there."

"I'm surprised she didn't tell you."

"Your cousin is good at what she does."

Haven smiled and nodded her head.

"Haven, you must know, if I didn't have to leave, I would stay."

"I understand," she said, taking his hand in hers. She turned it over and began tracing circles on his palm. "I'll miss these hands," she confessed.

"And I yours."

"I'll miss these lips," she said, bringing one of her fingers up to trace his mouth.

"And I yours."

"I'll miss this heart," she whispered, dropping her hand and placing her palm flat against his chest.

He tipped her face up to his and kissed her in response.

For as long as they dared, Haven and Colton shared this retreat. It was much like their time together. Rich, breathtaking, and more diminutive in span than either would have liked it to be.

Chapter Forty-One

Colton and Haven returned their horses to their stalls. Freshly bathed and rubbed down, the animals happily munched on their hay.

Almost on cue, the barn phone rang.

"That must be Moira," Haven said. "Would you mind picking it up?"

Colton answered the phone.

"Why aren't you answering your cell?" Moira asked in her typical style.

"Haven asked me to leave it behind."

"So, you've said your good-byes, then?"

"Yes."

"Do you want to leave as soon as I get there? Would that make it easier?"

"No. I think she'd benefit from some time with you before we head out."

"Okay. I've brought goodies."

Her mock cheerfulness did nothing to stop the hole in Colton's chest from spreading. "That sounds great," he answered, but there was no energy to his response. His words were hollow.

"I'll see you in a bit, okay?"

"See you then."

"Oh. Colton?"

"Yes, Moira."

"Levi's already been fired from a job."

"How is that even possible?"

"He decided it was okay to show up four hours late. John Stackton was having none of it."

"He's lucky John didn't punch him in the face."

"He did." Moira chuckled for a second, then clicked off after that.

Colton turned around to see that Haven was nowhere to be found. She was either off doing chores or allowing herself the cry she'd been fighting since they had left their little oasis at the edge of the farm.

Rather than go to the main house to check on her, Colton headed back to the bunkhouse to pack his stuff. Only after he was nearly done did he notice the cream envelope sitting atop his bed.

On the back, written across the seal, were instructions telling him to read it only after he had left.

Colton didn't listen.

He tore into the envelope as quickly as his fingers would allow, not noticing the paper cut such quick action gave nor its accompanying sting.

Colton,

I couldn't bear to watch you go. Thank you so much for all that you have done for me. All that you have done for Levi. I know it was you that got him the jobs he now has. Being in the movies is all he has ever wanted. And now, you've put your reputation on the line because he is related to me.

I must confess: I know you don't like my brother. I also know you think I don't know him. But I do. He isn't good like you. It's true. But he is family. And I am sure Moira has told you. Family means everything to me. It always has.

So, I've decided to go see my mom. It's been too

long. It was either that or spend the entire evening crying or begging you to stay.

The last time I was able to get one of the nurses on the phone, they told me she was doing better. It is time I go see her for myself. If what the nurse said is true, she may even be able to come home soon.

Her problems, as you know, are more mental than physical. They always have been. She still misses my dad. She never quite got over him.

Like I suspect I will never quite get over you.

I've thought a lot about what you said. It's true. My place is on the farm. And yours is making movies. Don't be mad. But I made Moira send me a few of your more notable films. I only recently watched them. I wanted to get to know you first.

You're good, by the way. But I suspect you already know that.

I wish there was a way I could make all of your money problems go away. The money I got from selling my mother's stocks isn't enough. I had Moira check for me. I also looked into selling a part of the farm. But it wouldn't be enough, I'm afraid. Plus, my cousin said you'd never forgive me if I did. I guess she's right. You put so much into helping me pay off my debts that it wouldn't be nice to decide to let some of the land go now. You might think I don't truly cherish it, which I do.

I love it, actually, like I love you, Colton.

It's hard to write those words. As I have learned, love changes very little in life. Or in my life, at least. I love you, and you will still leave. But I suppose, if we were different people, we wouldn't be able to love each other the way we do. One change invariably triggers another.

And I wouldn't want anything about you to be different. Everything you are, everything you've done in your past, brought you to me. I hope you can hold onto that in the dark times. I know we'll both have them.

So, it is with that in mind that I have decided not to curse the fates or to hate all of the hours that we are apart.

Love, even for a short time, is a gift. I won't be mad at the universe just because my epic romance was shorter than most.

I guess that's what I want you to understand most of all. No matter what happens. No matter how long we are apart, you must never forget one thing: You are the love of my life.

From the moment I first saw you, I knew.

Never forget that. And, please, if you can, never forget me.

Love,

Haven

Colton balled up Haven's letter in his fist. Then he slid to the floor, bent his knees to his chest, and rested his forehead on them.

Moira arrived to find him like that, sitting in the dark. "Colton? Are you okay?"

He didn't answer.

"I found this note tacked to the main house's front door. It says Haven left."

He nodded his head against his knees. Not a comforting gesture.

"Colton? Say something?"

He couldn't speak.

Moira saw the crumpled letter on the floor, a dot of

blood at the corner. She picked it up and scanned through it quickly. He didn't stop her.

"Colton, I'm so sorry."

"So am I," he finally answered.

Moira sat on the bed, waiting for him to speak. "Did you ever tell her?"

"About buying the farm? No."

"I think maybe…after reading this…wouldn't it help?"

"No. She'd feel indebted to me."

"By the sounds of this letter, she already does."

"Not as much as she would if she knew."

After a bit, Moira said, "I wish there was something I could do."

"You made it possible for me to meet her. I will be indebted to you for the rest of my life."

Moira shed a tear.

Colton raised his head at her sniffling. "Come on, Moira," he said. "Don't cry. You're not the crying type."

"I can't help it," she said. "It's you. You! Out of all of the people I know, you have fallen in love."

"Yep."

"And now you have to leave. It's like the plot out of some horribly sadistic romantic movie. The kind with the bad ending."

"Those aren't romances, Moira. They're called tragedies."

"Well, I think you deserve more than a tragedy. After everything you've done for her."

"It's the fact that she doesn't know that makes it so meaningful. If she'd said I was the love of her life after she knew I kept her brother from selling off her farm, it wouldn't mean as much."

Moira didn't argue. "Do you think we should get on the road? If she isn't here?"

"No. Someone has to feed the animals in the morning."

"The note she left me said she's arranged for someone to do that for the entire time she's gone."

"Oh," Colton responded.

"We could stay if you're not ready to leave."

"No. I'm ready."

"Do you want me to throw away this note?"

"No. I'll keep it. I only crumpled it up because I was angry. And sad."

"I understand," Moira said, smoothing out the pages against her thigh.

Colton grabbed the letter after she was done.

"You know, if you weren't going to keep it, I would have."

"Is that so?" Colton asked.

"Words like that you don't throw away."

It was when Colton muttered, "I don't need the note to remember what she said. Every word is imprinted on my heart forever," that Moira excused herself, probably to cry some more. She said it was only to grab the bag she'd left on the front porch of the main house before she'd known she wouldn't be staying the night, but he knew better.

Colton watched as his publicist's shadow crossed the yard, wishing it was another's coming the opposite way, back toward him.

Chapter Forty-Two

"Are you sure you don't want to see the world's largest jelly donut?" Moira asked.

"I'm sure," Colton said, staring out of the window of the truck that had brought him to Haven and her farm in the first place.

"But you've already passed up so many interesting options. World's largest papier mâché reindeer. World's largest rhinestone bumblebee. World's largest tote bag made from recycled materials."

"I don't think a bunch of potato sacks sewn together qualifies as a tote bag made from recycled materials."

"Repurposed, then. And it's as big as a residential street in California."

"And as interesting," Colton replied.

All of Moira's attempts to cheer Colton up had had little effect. She had managed to earn a few cheap laughs. But they'd been at the expense of some of her clients' more ridiculous stunts, all of which had hit the papers recently.

"Are you losing your edge?" Colton had asked after learning that one particularly quirky detail about a client's predilections had made prime time news.

"There's nothing I can do if he places an ad in the paper, using the name of the most famous character he's ever played as his pseudonym."

"Aren't pseudonyms just for authors?"

"It was a novel of an ad."

Colton had laughed against his will.

"And quite the novel ad. I don't think anyone has requested that particular combination of costumes or talents before."

"I would say not," Colton had replied before he'd fallen deaf once more.

Even the new Anna song clogging up the airwaves had done nothing to influence his mood one way or the other.

"Earth to Colton," Moira finally said.

Apparently, he'd zoned out. "You haven't found the world's silliest publicist, have you? I don't think we have to go far to see her."

"Ha ha ha," she responded. "No. I was just asking if you wanted to pull in somewhere for the night."

"I'd rather keep driving if that's okay with you."

"Colton, I'm not sure I can stay awake."

"I can take over. I'm wide awake."

"Are you sure?"

"Yes. There's no way I'm going to be getting any sleep. I'd rather get back to what I have to get back to if that's the case."

"You don't have to start filming for another week."

"I have a lot of stunt sequences to learn."

"You better not injure yourself on this set. The loans you've taken out against what you'll be paid have a high interest rate."

"Don't remind me," he said.

Moira pulled over at the next gas station and went inside to use the restroom while he pumped gas.

Colton was going back to a whole lot of nothing.

All of the belongings he hadn't sold were in storage, mainly a few pieces of movie memorabilia that he couldn't quite part with, a heap of free clothes from designers, a selection of books, all of his DVDs, a few random kitchen appliances plus utensils, and three of the movie industry's lesser known awards, given to him for Best Kiss in the Rain, Best Verbal Comeback, and Best Slow Walk Away from a Huge, Fiery Explosion. Lesser known awards indeed.

Colton's house had fetched quite the price though. So, that had been nice. Moira had done all she could to ratchet up the attention. Some new playboy would be seducing women in the bungalow in no time. It was practically built for it.

Colton, on the other hand, was officially done with his days of seduction. He no longer wanted to lie to young women or to himself.

All he could think about was finishing the movies he'd promised to finish and seeing Haven again. One day. If she was not already happily married to some new guy.

Four years is a long time. Anything can happen in four years.

"I've bought you four herbal teas. Each is supposed to awaken the senses in one way or another."

"No caffeine. I got it."

"I don't think showing up jittery will help your cause."

"I know," he responded. "And I appreciate your attention to detail."

"I just hope you'll appreciate my snoring. I am about to pass out."

Colton told Moira he was going to run in to use the

restroom, then he'd be right back. By the time he returned, she was fast asleep. He shouldn't have, but he checked her phone when he heard it vibrate in the cup holder next to his.

Please forgive me.

The message was from Haven. She was asking for Moira's forgiveness for bailing on her. Colton knew his publicist well enough to understand that there was no need for Haven to apologize. Moira was just as moved by Haven's letter as he was.

It was impossible for anybody to be mad at someone who could write something as sweet as what she'd written. Even a cynic like the one sawing logs next to him.

The woman wasn't lying. She is exhausted. And she'll snore if she wants to.

Colton laughed at his own joke. Somebody had to.

Chapter Forty-Three

"Moira," Colton said, shaking her gently. "We're here."

"Wait. Hold on. What?" Her words came out in a rush. Colton's publicist was completely out of it. "Where are we again?" she asked, rubbing her eyes.

"Your house."

"What time is it?"

"Time to get inside," he said, registering the click of photog shutters even from a distance.

"What's the—" Then Moira heard it, too. She immediately flew into publicist mode. "Put your jacket on over your head."

"It's too late," Colton replied. "They've already gotten what they need."

"How did they know?"

"I'll give you one guess."

"Levi," they said at the same time.

Moira checked her messages. She had been receiving texts and phone calls all night. But she'd slept like the dead.

Colton hadn't checked any of what had come through after he'd seen the message from Haven. He couldn't. He'd felt guilty for reading a private communication. And he hadn't been able to get over the fact that she hadn't texted him, too.

The distance, though new, was nearly unbearable.

If he hadn't been saddled with a rather large loan to pay back, he would have dropped out of his next film. He wanted to be around no one and nothing.

The moment after getting back from Haven's would have been the best time for him to do one of those reality shows where the contestant was transported by a helicopter to the middle of the Amazon and forced to find a way out on his own. There was nothing like survival to take your mind off the affairs of the heart.

Once safely inside of Moira's, Colton made himself at home on her couch. She'd always had a nice place. Not as lavish as the bachelor pad he had just sold. But whenever he'd been here, it had always felt like home.

He'd spent more than his fair share of nights sleeping on this couch. After being dumped by Anna, he'd barely been able to function. Then, after that, Moira had tried to dry him out several times on her own, back when she was sure his problem wasn't as bad as it actually was. None of her interventions had stuck, of course. Not until she'd involved her cousin.

"I'm just going to take a nap."

Moira waved to him, signaling that whatever he wanted to do was okay.

Colton fell into a restless sleep. Snippets of his time on the farm with Haven flashed in and out of his mind. As did images of Levi going back to harm his sister. When Moira woke him, it was dark outside.

"Shit," he muttered. "What time is it?"

"It's nearly ten o'clock."

"I was supposed to check in with the producers."

"I already did that."

"What did you tell them?"

"That you were exhausted, but as dry as dry can be."

"Thanks, Moira," he said, running his fingers through his hair.

"Listen, Colton," she said hesitantly. "I don't mean to be rude, but you could use a shower."

He laughed at her comment. "I'm sure I could."

"Well, feel free to take one any time you like."

"I was planning on checking into a hotel."

"There's no need. You can stay here."

"Why? I get a free room as part of my contract."

"About that…" Moira hesitated.

"Please tell me they didn't cut me from the film."

"No. They didn't."

"Well, what, then?"

"I negotiated a raise for you."

"Wow. That's great. How did you do it?"

"I may have promised that you'd stay here where I could keep an eye on you."

"Ahhh. I see. They still don't trust me."

"Not exactly."

"But they know about your reputation?"

"Yes. Apparently, some people consider me to be a bit of a hard-ass."

"Well, you did force George onto a helicopter even though he's deathly afraid of flying and of heights."

"And the stories about him have died down, have they not?" she countered.

"Also, you sent me to live on a farm out in the middle of nowhere."

"And you're sober."

"Plus, Geoffrey isn't allowed anywhere near a

biscuit or tea."

"Hey. That's not fair. The doctors said—" But Moira stopped when she saw that Colton was laughing. "What?" she asked. "What's so funny?"

"You," Colton answered.

"I beg your pardon."

"For all of your tough exterior, your no-holds-barred attitude, you really do care."

Moira shrugged in response.

"I appreciate that about you," he said, laying a hand on her shoulder, squeezing it once. "I really do."

"You're one to talk," Moira muttered when she thought her client was out of earshot.

It was true. No matter his joking, he did care. If he didn't, he wouldn't be in his current predicament.

Chapter Forty-Four

Colton was woken up by Moira's cell phone ringing on the kitchen counter.

"Can you get that, please?" she called from the other room. "Pretend you're my assistant."

"As if anyone will buy that," Colton chided, getting up and grabbing his publicist's cell phone anyway.

"Moira's dutiful assistant," he answered. He should have checked the number.

"Colton?" Haven asked.

He didn't respond, just hung up.

"Who was that?" Moira questioned, emerging in a bathrobe with a towel in hand, drying her hair.

"It was your cousin." His tone was flat, dead.

"Haven just called?"

"Yes," he answered.

"Then why did you hang up?"

"I don't know," he said.

The sound of her voice had been like a blade through his chest. He hadn't been able to focus. He would never be able to, not while dreaming of a life that could never be his.

"I'd better call her back," Moira said.

"Can you take the call into the other room?" he asked.

As soon as Moira had closed the door to her

bedroom, he threw on some running shoes. Then he was out the door. He didn't care that there were photogs stationed all around the neighborhood, documenting his every move. Even with the blinds drawn and the car parked strategically in front of the house, thereby making it hard to see through the glass panels on either side of the foyer door, they always seemed to know when someone was coming or going.

I guess that's what they get paid for, Colton thought to himself.

At first, Colton's muscles were tight, used to riding more than running. After a bit, they loosened up. Colton jogged down the long street to the cul-de-sac. Then he let himself out of the gate into the little bit of woods that the residences shared. It wasn't much, but it reminded him of the place Haven had shown him before she'd taken off.

It wasn't as pretty. But it was still cozy and unexpected. Just like the place he would always think of as theirs. When he was ready, he decided to head back to the road. Once there, he jogged up the hill, past Moira's house, then down another street. A few faces he recognized from their behind-the-scenes work on movies registered his identity. They waved. Colton waved back.

I need to be my normal self.

My best self, he corrected quickly.

It was true. If he had any hope of getting his financial life back in order, he needed to improve not only his work ethic, but his reputation. He had to work harder and faster and better than he had ever worked in his life. And smile all the while he was doing it.

Colton had to be Mr. Nice Guy, the actor all

directors went to when they wanted to ensure that the investments of those footing the bill would be returned tenfold at the box office.

As he jogged, Colton formulated a plan. He would amp up his public appearances. He would attend colleagues' movie premieres, put in a little face time. Enough to keep his fans interested. Not so much that he oversaturated the market.

He would be smart for once rather than willful and ungrateful. Not many people were given the types of chances he'd already been given. He had no business spending his time moping about something that was never meant to be, not for the long term anyway.

When Colton got back to Moira's, he was drenched in sweat. "Don't worry. I'm going to take a shower," he called when he saw Moira's look of horror.

"It's not that," she began. But she couldn't complete her sentence.

"Moira. What's wrong?"

He settled her into a side chair in the living room. "Please. Tell me what's wrong?"

"Colton, there's been an accident."

His head immediately started spinning. "Is it Haven?" he demanded. "Is she okay?" His hands were around Moira's arms, gripping a little too hard. Noticing this, he took a step back. "Moira, please. Tell me what's happened."

"Haven's mother is dead."

With that, the life drained out of him. This would kill Haven. And he couldn't go back to check on her. He had to start filming.

"Moira, can you get me out of—"

"I already tried," she said. "My hands are tied."

"Can you go…?" he asked.

"I've booked my flight. I leave in a couple hours."

"How did it happen?"

"She fell out of a window."

She jumped, Colton thought. But he didn't have the heart to say it out loud. "Haven didn't sound—"

"She didn't know earlier, when she called and you hung up. It happened while I was on the phone with her."

"She saw her mother jump…I mean, fall out of a window?" Colton felt devastated.

"No. A nurse told her while we were on the phone. Right after she had finished telling me how well her mother was doing."

"I think I'm going to be sick."

"I know, Colton. I'm so sorry."

"Tell her I'd be there if I could."

"I will."

"Do you think they will let me attend the funeral?"

"There isn't going to be a funeral."

That made sense. Haven's mother hadn't left her house in years except for medical treatment. Nothing was sadder than a funeral unless it was one that no one attended.

"Is Levi going?"

"I don't know."

"Don't let him—"

"I won't," Moira assured, placing a gentle hand on his forearm. "Levi won't hurt her."

"Moira, I know this sounds indecent. But was everything in order…before…? Is there any way that he can—"

"The contracts we drew up for the sale prevented

her mother from ever signing over power of attorney again if only because he would lose his money if he ever accepted such an offer."

"I didn't know you could do such a thing until you—"

"I know," she stated. "I learn from the best. Haven's portion of everything can never be touched. He can't even take the money if she wanted to give it to him."

"Thank you, Moira. Really."

"You're welcome." Moira excused herself to begin packing and making the calls she needed to make.

Colton grabbed his stuff and headed to the guest bathroom. He needed to shower and have time to think. He didn't know what to say. He had to come up with exactly the right thing.

As he scrubbed at his skin, hot water running over his flesh, Colton imagined Haven's eyes, sad and misty. The despair that had to be in them now. The fear.

She was truly on her own. And he was stuck here, a thousand miles away, learning how to pretend to fight so a bunch of cinephiles wouldn't say the action sequences looked too cheesy.

*If only I could...*Before he could think better of it, Colton rushed out of the shower. "Moira, wait," he called. "I'm coming with you." Hearing nothing and fearing she was silently disagreeing with him, he added, "The director can just deal. I won't miss the first day of shooting."

Colton knocked on Moira's bedroom door. There was no answer. He opened the door only to find that there was no one there. He checked her closet, also nothing. He knocked on her bathroom door, then eased it open. Nada.

The house was empty.

Where did you...

On the kitchen counter was his answer. A note. In Moira's handwriting.

Dear Colton,

I know you'll find this once you realize I have gone. I'm sorry. I left for the airport early because Haven asked me to come alone. She specifically said not to bring you.

It's just the pain. She only wants to be with family right now. Please don't be upset.

Moira

Chapter Forty-Five

Colton couldn't oblige.

There was nothing to be but upset when a person left a note like that for you.

He'd begun to think of himself as intimately tied to Haven, the kind of connected that goes beyond friendship, the kind that goes beyond the boundaries of nascent couples. The kind that allows you into hospital rooms and behind the scenes of family tragedies.

I guess I was wrong, he thought to himself.

Wrapped in a towel, Colton paced. Then he sat on Moira's couch. Then he paced some more.

He couldn't find anything to do with his hands, with his feet, with his body. His legs were restless, his mind leading him in a thousand different directions.

He would have set out for a run, except he'd just had one.

He thought about texting Haven, telling her he was sorry. But she wouldn't want that. If she didn't want him to come to comfort her, he doubted she would want to hear anything from him at all.

Colton stood up so he could grab some clothes and get busy doing nothing. Except he had no intention of respecting what was written in that note. He was going back to see Haven. He had to. He wouldn't be able to live with himself if he didn't.

Quickly, Colton got on the line and called a friend

he had on set. "Jack, listen. I need a favor," he said.

Jack listened intently as Colton told him what was going on. He promised to email him the sequences that Colton was to learn and to arrange some extra practice for when he got back.

"I owe you one," Colton said, then hung up the phone. *Haven. I'm on my way. No matter what you may have said, I know you need me. Now more than ever.*

Chapter Forty-Six

"Are you sure you wouldn't like a drink?" the stewardess asked for the umpteenth time.

"I'm recently sober," Colton finally replied.

The lady next to him suddenly had some input she'd like to share on the matter. "You don't know what you're missing," she said, raising her Bloody Mary.

"Actually, I do. That's why I had to quit."

"You know, my sister had to quit for a bit," she stated. "It didn't take."

Colton didn't say anything else for the remainder of the flight. Not when the very spoiled child sitting behind him kicked his seat for the billionth time. Not when the woman next to him spilled alcohol down his shirt and all over his pants. Not when the stewardess who obviously recognized him tried to dry his nether region with an airline-issued towel.

Colton simply waved away the apologies and grabbed the towel intended to be of aid so he could do the drying himself. Luckily, his flightmate had switched to straight vodka after her fourth Bloody Mary, making the cleaning-up process a bit easier.

When the plane arrived at its destination, Colton couldn't get out of the cabin fast enough. He grabbed his carry-on bag and rushed through the terminal to the rental car service. The farm was still a distance away. It would take him several hours to get there.

As he was accepting the keys for one of the last cars left on the lot and heading in the direction of the space in which the car was purported to be parked, Colton received a text.

Just arrived at Haven's, it read.

The flight Moira was on had been full. Otherwise, he would have been on it, note be damned. Colton typed in a good-luck-and-take-care message, thinking it was probably for the best that her flight had been full.

Otherwise, he would have had to suffer through Moira's arguments, telling him that he shouldn't have come.

For the entire flight.

In much the same manner that she'd warned him against falling for her cousin or making her cousin fall for him.

Car found, key in the ignition, Colton pulled out of the lot at lightning speed only to find that the gas tank was only a quarter full. He quickly located a gas station, pulled in, paid for his gas with cash, and grabbed a few lightly caffeinated, sugar-infused drinks plus a bag of chips.

My new studio-assigned fitness instructor will love me for these choices.

Months on the farm had kept him in shape. But Colton hadn't done any real sculpting exercises in quite awhile.

The makeup artists will have to work a little bit harder, that's all. They shouldn't mind. It's what they're paid for.

Once the tank was full, Colton hit the road. His phone vibrated again. It was Moira. It had to be. Colton glanced at the screen.

Colton? Where are you? You aren't answering your cell or the phone at my house.

He pulled over so he could respond. The last thing Haven needed was for Moira to be worried about him.

I'm fine, he typed furiously. *I'll be available in a couple hours. Anything you need until then?*

No, she answered.

How's Haven?

Not good. I wish I had brought you with me.

He typed, *I'm coming*, before deleting it. He didn't want Haven to know. *Keep me updated*, he sent instead.

Will do, she responded.

Then Colton pulled back onto the highway, vowing not to stop driving until he was at Haven's side once more.

Chapter Forty-Seven

The road went on for what seemed like forever. Seconds felt like minutes, minutes like hours, hours like days. No music existed that could distract Colton from the painful distance that separated him from Haven.

He didn't know what he'd say when he arrived. He hoped Haven would simply fall into his arms. But she might not be happy to see him. Grief did strange things to people.

Like making them ask relatives to keep you away.

Jake had texted several times. Colton hadn't read the messages. But he was pretty sure they involved updates on how he could get back into his director's and producers' good graces.

To be honest, Colton didn't really care.

Fifteen minutes from Haven's, his palms began to sweat. His stomach churned. He didn't want to see what he knew he'd find. An empty shell where his love used to be.

In the driveway, he parked the car so it wasn't visible from the kitchen window. Then he walked to the main house. As was often the case, the front door was open, the screen the only barrier between what was inside and the outside world.

Colton took one final breath then pulled open the screen door.

"Haven," he called.

The air turned electric.

"Colton," Moira answered.

"Yeah," he responded, "uh, I finally made it."

"Colton, I said…" Her voice trailed off when he rounded the corner.

Haven sat on the couch, staring down at her hands. Her cheeks were stained with tears. Her fingers fiddled with each other because they had nothing else to do.

"Haven?" he asked, "are you okay?"

She shook her head.

"Haven, I am so sorry. So very, very sorry."

"Good day," Levi interrupted.

The sight of Haven's no good brother was enough to send Colton into a rage. Haven didn't need to be dealing with such a prick at a time like this.

"Levi, could you give us a minute?" Haven asked, her voice barely audible.

"Sure," he barked, slamming down his beer.

Already drinking.

Colton made eye contact with Moira. The question he sent through the air: *Are his other projects going okay?*

Her answer: a silent shake of her head.

Even a smorgasbord of opportunities placed right in his lap was too little for the fool. Everything had to be done for him. He was a leech. A parasite.

But Colton needed to focus on Haven now, not his hatred for her brother. "Haven?" The question: *Can I come closer? Can I hold you?*

She nodded her head.

In a second, Colton was at her side, taking her into his arms.

Moira politely excused herself and headed into the

kitchen. To read Levi the riot act most likely.

"I am sorry, Haven," Colton said. "So very sorry. If there is anything I can do, please let me know."

"I think you've done enough." Her tone had an edge to it.

He pulled back, looked at her face. She was angry. "Are you mad at me for coming?"

She shook her head.

"But you are mad?"

She nodded her head.

"I'm not sure I understand."

"I wasn't ready to see you."

"Why?" he asked.

She heaved a huge sigh, then stood, taking him by the hand, pulling him out through the door, toward the barn. The pressure of her palm kept him glued to her.

Once under the heavy rafters they had spent so much time beneath, she began saddling Cicero. When he didn't immediately start getting his mount ready, she signaled him to grab Ol' Faithful and do the same. Colton obeyed. He wasn't sure what was going on, but he would do whatever he was told, for as long as it took.

Dawn was just breaking when they set out. He'd been forced to wait too many hours for his flight to Idaho. He hadn't been able to make it before now.

Luckily, there would soon be enough light to ride by.

In one quick movement, Haven was atop her golden gelding. She sent him into a canter from a dead stop. Once they had cleared the barn, she was galloping. They rode the pathway between the fields until they got to the gate at the far end of the largest pasture. Haven unlatched it in one swift motion.

Colton knew where they were going. To the place she had shown him before he left. He didn't say anything, just watched her body for signs that she was about to break as they raced to a message he wasn't sure he wanted to hear.

Once they reached their destination, Haven dismounted. She walked Cicero a bit until he was cool enough to be secured to a nearby tree. Colton followed suit, tying Ol' Faithful near her stablemate.

Haven slipped into the copse of trees. Colton did as well. Once again, the majority of the day's light was blocked out. It was just them, this garden oasis, and whatever it was Haven wished to share.

"I know," she said, settling herself down upon a rock.

Colton didn't follow. He wasn't sure he wanted to. "You know what?" he asked.

"I know what you did."

Colton gulped.

"You risked your future to save my farm."

He could have lied. But lying wouldn't have gotten him anywhere. "Yes," he finally admitted.

"You took a loan out against your upcoming salary."

"Who told you?"

"It isn't important."

He begged to differ.

"Colton, how could you?" She was more sad than angry now.

"I had to," was his answer.

"Why?"

"Because I love you. And you love this farm."

Tears were brimming in her eyes. "I can never repay you."

"You already have," he said, scooting closer.

She smiled a sad smile. "Why didn't you tell me?"

"Because I didn't want you to feel like this. Guilty. Indebted. You owe me nothing, Haven."

"I don't agree," she countered. "But I won't argue the point any further. Not now anyway."

He nodded. "How are you?" he asked, tracing her face with his fingertips.

"Not good," she said.

"No one expects you to be…"

But she cut him off. "I didn't want you to see me like this."

"Why?" He couldn't keep the confusion from his face.

"Since the first day I met you, I have been a mess. Financially underwater. Consumed with worry. Crying at every new development in my life. Tied to two relatives"—her voice cracked on this part—"who weren't or aren't able to kick their demons."

"Your mother loved you," he interrupted.

"I know," she said. When he didn't say anything else, she added, "And, once again, it wasn't enough."

"Oh, Haven. That's not true."

"She killed herself, Colton."

"I suspected…"

"The report said she accidentally tripped, fell through the window…but I know. She threw herself through it."

"Haven, I'm so sorry."

"Everybody is," she admitted. "But that won't bring her back."

"No," he agreed. "It won't."

"The worst part was she was lucid. Right before she took her own life, she was as lucid as she has been in years. She was talking about making changes. She told me she loved me. Said she was sorry that I had been left to deal with everything, including Levi."

"So, she knew about Levi?"

Haven nodded. "I told her that he'd had a lucky break, gotten some jobs in the movies."

Colton smiled.

"She patted my hand. Then, a nurse came in to do some checks, see how she was feeling, give her a dose of meds."

Colton listened intently.

"I wasn't gone long."

"Oh, Haven…"

"But she was gone. By the time I got back to her room, she was gone." Haven collapsed into a fit of tears, her face against his chest.

Colton stroked her hair, whispered *shh*, and said it would all be okay. One day. Though he wasn't sure he believed his promise. Colton had never loved his family as much as Haven loved hers. He wasn't sure many people could or did.

"I'm sorry I told Moira to keep you away," she apologized.

"It's okay," he said.

"I just couldn't face you…knowing everything you'd done."

"Like I said, it's okay. You are entitled to feel any way you feel. To do anything you want to do."

"Are you in trouble?" Haven asked, cutting him off, more worried about him now than she was herself.

"In trouble for what?"

"For coming here. Shouldn't you be filming a movie?"

"I have a man on the inside," he responded. "I've worked it out."

"You didn't quit, did you?"

"No. No. Nothing like that. I'm only skipping rehearsals."

"They do rehearsals for movies?"

"It's not like a play, but, yes, sort of."

Haven blinked back a new wave of tears. "I seem to cause trouble wherever I go."

"Haven," Colton said, putting his hands on her shoulders and willing her to look up at him.

She did.

"None of this is because of you. Not your mother. Not Levi. Not the farm. You haven't done any of this."

"I messed up your life. You are in debt because of me."

"No. I made my choices. You never asked me for a thing."

"But you felt bad—"

"I did what I've done out of love, not guilt. You deserve better. And I found a way to give it to you."

"You sold your house," she argued.

"I would have done so anyway. Too many bad memories."

"You've had to move in with Moira…so you can pay back your loans quicker."

So his publicist had finally cracked. She was the one who had told Haven. Not Levi. He couldn't possibly know about the details of Colton's contract.

"Moira negotiated a better deal for me. That's why

I'm living with her. I'm not completely destitute."

"It's all my fault," she cried again.

"No, Haven. It's not. I will not let you say that again." Once she settled, he continued. "You've changed my life. Helped me get off drugs and alcohol. Taught me the value of truly hard work."

She smiled a little.

"Taught me to love," he said, tracing the side of her face.

She looked up at him. "You taught me to love, too," she said.

Colton pulled Haven to him. For a bit, they held each other, Haven providing him with as much comfort as he was giving her. Even when she had nothing, she still managed to give him her all.

"I love you," she whispered when everything had gone silent, when neither could hear the birds in the trees anymore.

"I love you, too," he answered, more certain of those words than anything he had ever been in his whole life.

Chapter Forty-Eight

The next few days were filled with tears and promises and the removal of Levi from Haven's life. A drunken fight in which Levi blamed their mother's death on Haven had given Colton the opportunity he had been waiting for since the moment Levi had first shown up at the farm. Colton had picked Haven's sorry excuse for a brother up by the collar and escorted him off the premises.

Moira had smiled while her client had taken out the trash.

Haven had sighed her first sigh of relief in days.

When it was time to leave for the airport, Colton only went reluctantly, promising he would be back to check on Haven as soon as he could.

Per her most famous client's suggestion, Moira agreed to work from Haven's farm for a couple weeks, while Colton battened down the hatches at Moira's place.

His first day of shooting went better than expected. Though the art director was none too pleased with his lack of six-pack abs, he had nothing to say about his biceps. Arranging feedbags and fixing fences had been enough to give him the "smokin' guns" the little man was looking for.

The fight sequences were very similar to those from another movie Colton had done a few years back.

Same choreographer, so it had come as no surprise. Everyone had their style.

Before he knew it, the first shoot flew by. Colton was able to visit Haven twice, each for two days at a time. A red-eye took him out to Idaho, and a red-eye took him back. The director rearranged the schedule a bit so he could shoot scenes for which Colton was not to look his best on the day after the picture's leading man returned. He was a fan of the method approach.

The second movie went well, too. It wasn't long until Colton was back in the black. He paid off his loan with interest and bought a small place of his own. This time, it was an apartment with enough furnishings to keep him going. Nothing extravagant. Nothing showy.

By the third film, Colton was doing press for the first. It had been billed as the blockbuster of the season. Luckily, all of the media hype didn't end with the fans being let down. Instead, word of mouth had spread, and the film doubled its original projected earnings to become one of the top-earning films of all time.

The shoots for the second and third movies in the series were greenlit almost immediately.

Through it all, Colton made as much time for Haven as he could. She, in turn, did the same for him. It took a while, but Haven eventually returned to a semblance of her old self. Cicero was still going strong and, with him, Haven's attachment to the farm.

So when Colton found himself at yet another premiere, this time for an indie film that Moira had assured him had the potential to increase his award-show credibility, Colton was surprised to see a familiar face standing just past the red carpet.

Dutifully, he gave brief interview after brief

interview until he could make his way over to her.

"Haven," he said, taking the sight of her in. She was dressed in a long burgundy gown with rhinestone detail. She looked more gorgeous than every leading lady he had ever starred opposite put together.

"Hi," she greeted him.

Immediately, photogs' cameras started flashing. They didn't know who she was, but they were certain this meeting was important.

"Mr. Grey," a familiar voice called out, that of Sun Daily, the woman who had once tried to track him down while he was getting sober. He ignored her.

"It's nice to see you," he said to Haven. It was as though he hadn't talked to her in weeks even though it had only been hours. Their last communication was via text.

"It's nice to see you, too," she mimicked.

He leaned in and gave her a kiss on the cheek. He was unwilling for anything else to make the gossip magazines.

"I've been thinking," she said against the scruff of his cheek.

"*In the Know* readers now prefer scruff," he recalled Moira saying.

"Colton?"

"Yes," he answered, snapping back to the present. This entire moment seemed so surreal that his brain couldn't handle it. He had never imagined having Haven here, among the people he worked with, standing atop a red carpet, looking like she did now.

"I was wondering…"

Colton gulped.

"Would you marry me?"

He stared at her wide-eyed. From beyond the velvet ropes, he heard a few ladies gasp. Another few spoke some very unkind words about Haven. Green was not the best color on anybody, it turned out.

"Well?" she asked, interrupting his reverie.

"Did you just ask me to marry you?" he questioned.

"Yes," she replied breathily.

She was more nervous than he realized. A quick check of the obvious pulse knocking at the flesh of her neck revealed that her heart, too, was hammering in its chest.

Yet her demeanor was so cool, so calm, so collected.

"Colton?"

"Hmm," he said, imagining their wedding day, their wedding night, their children.

"Would you mind answering?" She looked nervous.

After all of this time, she still didn't get how special she was to him. If he was unkind, he would have dragged out the moment a bit. But he still wasn't able to cause her even mock harm.

"Yes," he answered.

"Is that yes, you would mind answering, or yes to my question?"

"Both," he replied, then bent down on one knee. "Haven," he said, misty eyes looking into her brilliant ones. "Would you marry me?"

She nodded her head as he launched himself back up and into her arms.

"Where's the ring?" a few onlookers shouted.

Haven and Colton ignored them. Theirs had never

been a traditional love affair. Their engagement didn't need to be either.

A few minutes later, a buzz emanated from Haven's evening clutch.

"Who is it?" Colton asked.

"No one," Haven responded without even looking.

"It can't be no one. Aren't you going to check?"

Haven shook her head.

"Give it to me," he commanded, a smile on his face.

"Not a chance, Mr. Grey."

"Are they fighting?" a fan called. "Already?"

"Haven, let me see your phone."

Reluctantly, she handed it over. There, on the bright screen, was a question. *What did he say?*

Moira, of course, was the sender. She'd known he was going to get engaged tonight. She'd known and she'd said nothing.

"I'm going to kill your cousin," Colton said upon seeing the message.

"No, you're not," Haven confidently replied.

"Oh?" he asked. "Why not?"

"Because you love her like you love me."

"In a different way," he said.

"In a much different way," Haven agreed, kissing him on the mouth despite the presence of so many witnesses.

After they'd tasted each other a bit, Colton pulled back. "You know, she never did feed me to the lions at the San Diego Zoo."

Just then, Haven's phone vibrated again. Colton looked down. Moira's age-old threat stared up at him from the screen.

If he says no, tell him I will feed him to the lions at the San Diego Zoo, testicles first.

I said yes, he replied. *And so did she.*

Moira typed only a question mark in return.

Colton ignored her. This part of his life, she could read about in the papers. It would be nice for her to discover a positive fact about her client, printed in black and white, that she hadn't had to spin or create herself.

"What do you say we get out of here?" Colton asked.

"Where are we going?"

"It's a secret," he answered.

"Colton, I know nothing about this city. You can tell me, and I still won't have a clue."

"Let's just say, I have a few oases of my own," he added.

Tomorrow, they would be in Hawaii. The next day they would be married. Colton had no desire to waste even another second as a single man. Not when Haven was his bride-to-be and their life together was the one he was born to discover.

As far as he was concerned, it was high time that he and Haven began living their happily ever after.

A word about the author...

Savannah Addison is a voracious reader, film junkie, and lover of all things romance. She believes time is best spent in the grip of a good story, either on the page or on screen. Visit Savannah at
www.savannahaddison.com